FREAKY FACTS about
NATURAL DISASTERS

Kathleen Duey
and
Mary Barnes

Aladdin Paperbacks

New York London Toronto Sydney Singapore

First Aladdin Paperbacks edition June 2000

Copyright © 2000 by Kathleen Duey and Mary Barnes

Aladdin Paperbacks
An imprint of Simon & Schuster
Children's Publishing Division
1230 Avenue of the Americas
New York, NY 10020

All rights reserved, including the right of
reproduction in whole or in part in any form.
Designed by Steve Scott
The text for this book was set in Bembo.
Printed and bound in the United States of America
10 9 8 7 6 5 4 3 2

Library of Congress Cataloging-in-Publication Data
Duey, Kathleen; Barnes, Mary A.
Freaky facts about natural disasters / by Kathleen Duey and Mary Barnes.
—1st Aladdin Paperbacks ed.
p.   cm
Summary: Presents true stories about nature run amok, describing tornadoes, blizzards, floods, lightning, dust storms, and other natural phenomena.
ISBN 0-689-82818-7
[1. Natural disasters—Juvenile literature. 2. Natural disasters.] I. Title
GB5019.B37 2000
CIP
AC

chapter one

TORNADOES

imagine this . . .

It's May and springtime is in full bloom on your family's farm. The days are warm and the nights are mild. The corn is a foot tall, the hay crop is doing well, and most of the cows have already dropped their calves.

There's always work to be done on the farm—but no one can work outside this afternoon. It's too stormy. Lightning flashes and thunder rolls through the valley. Rain drums at the roof. It started raining about an hour ago and it's still coming down too hard to do anything outside. You are stretched out on the couch, reading a book. This is the best part of having a thunderstorm today—you get to put off chores for a while.

Your younger brothers are in their room, playing Monopoly. You can hear them arguing once in a while, even over the racket and roar of the storm. Your mother is in the kitchen, an apron over her field clothes. Before the storm rolled in, she was driving one of the flatbed trucks, hauling hay to the cattle in the north pasture. The rain forced her inside, too. Now she is making tonight's supper.

Your father has taken the family pickup truck into town to buy lay mash for the chickens and a bag of fertilizer for your mother's peach trees.

You can hear the wind in the cottonwoods that shade the porch. Lightning flickers again and the thunder crashes, close enough to shake the ground. You prop up on one elbow to see through the kitchen door. Your mother has stopped working, an anxious frown on her face as she gazes out the window. The phone rings. She doesn't answer it. Picking up the phone with lightning hitting this close would be dangerous. It rings twice more, then stops.

The lightning crackles brightly, then fades, and flashes blue white again. Each time the thunder is a little farther behind the flash of light, a little less loud. In a few minutes, the worst of the storm seems to have passed and you can concentrate on your book again. As you read, the rain softens to a patter on the roof.

"Maybe it's over," your mother calls from the kitchen. "I just hope it didn't hurt the new corn too badly."

You frown. "Me, too, Mom." Then you turn a page in the book and hope that she will leave you alone for a while. When the rain stops completely, you'll have to go finish cleaning the chicken coop.

"Oh, no."

Your mother says it quietly, but something in the

tone of her voice makes you close the book and sit up.

"Come look at this," she says.

When you get to the kitchen, she is in front of the window, her eyes fixed on the sky outside. There is an odd quality to the clouds, a clotted texture. As you stand beside your mother and watch, she wipes her hands on a dishtowel, then lays it on the counter beside the casserole she's been making, never taking her eyes off the sky.

An odd, transparent shape appears below the belly of the clouds, then disappears. You hear your mother take in a quick breath. "Go get your brothers. Now."

For a second, you can't move, watching the whirling cloud form again and bulge downward as though it were heavy, then shrink and disappear again. It almost looks like distant sheets of rain, but you know it isn't. There is a weird, muted roar rising in the distance.

"Hurry up!" Your mother nudges you sharply. "Get your brothers into the storm cellar."

You run toward your brothers' room. You bump your shoulder on the door frame and stumble. They look up, startled. "Tornado!" you shout. "We have to get to the root cellar."

"Where's Mom and Dad?" your youngest brother wants to know as you hustle them down the hall.

"Dad's in town. Mom will come down with us." You

realize that you have to scream to be heard. The roaring has suddenly swelled to fill the world.

"Mom!" you shriek as you pass the kitchen. She is no longer in front of the window. She emerges from the dining room, clutching something against her chest. You recognize the family album full of pictures of you and your brothers from babyhood on. The roaring is too loud now for speech, and when you open the back door, the wind whips it wide, jerking you forward so hard your hand aches.

Outside, you grab your brothers by their collars and hang on to them as your mother struggles to raise the cellar door. She fights her apron, which writhes like a live thing in the wind, whipping up and covering her face until she can untie it and let it go. For an instant you watch it rise like a bird, then you push your brothers ahead of you and reach for your mother's trembling hand. As the wind slashes at your face you fight to stay calm, praying that your father will see the tornado and manage to avoid it, that you will get the cellar door latched down in time—that it will hold. . . .

FREAKY (BUT TRUE!) FACTS

Many people who live in "Tornado Alley" have "fraidy holes" in the ground—root cellars with room for two to four people, with doors installed over them. During the terrible 1999 tornado in Oklahoma, one family fit 16 people and a dog into a shelter that had been built for four. They all lived, but it took three men to hold the door shut against the force of the wind.

After the 1999 Oklahoma tornado a state trooper saw what looked like a rag doll covered with mud, stuck in a tree. When he pulled it free, it started crying—the rag doll was really a ten-month-old baby girl who had been ripped from her mother's arms by the tornado. She recovered.

In Bridgecreek, Oklahoma in 1999, houses were splintered. One woman had a 1 x 2 board wind-driven through her head—in the right ear, out the other shoulder. Amazingly, she survived.

After a tornado, it is common to see straw sticking out of tree trunks and fence posts. After a 1915 tornado, an iron water hydrant was found full of splinters pushed right into the metal!

A tornado in McComb, Mississippi, tossed three 40-passenger school buses—fortunately empty—into the woods near a school. All three buses cleared an eight-foot embankment!

In 1896, near Des Moines, Iowa, a tornado drove a steel rail from the railroad 15 feet into the ground! In 1091, after England's earliest recorded tornado, 26-foot-long church roof rafters were driven about 22 feet into the earth.

In the 1999 Oklahoma tornado, an airplane wing torn from a plane at the Chickasha airport was found in Moore, 50 miles away.

After a tornado partly destroyed a commercial dog kennel, a missing dog was found a half mile away in the top of a tree—amazingly, uninjured.

Tornadoes have driven pencils and spoons into brick walls. A steel can was pierced by a splinter. A broomstick was found driven through a utility pole.

A basketball backboard ended up only five feet above the ground when a tornado bent the heavy metal pipe it was mounted on.

The south wall of a grocery store was blown down, leaving shelves and canned goods that had been standing against it, unmoved. Another tornado destroyed a home, leaving crystal brandy snifters intact. A third twister smashed a house to rubble except for one kitchen cupboard. It was carried away and then set down gently, all the dishes intact.

In Claude, Texas, a huge oak tree was uprooted and dragged through a brick garage. The bricks were scattered all over the neighborhood, but the two cars in the garage were unharmed.

In Iowa in 1994, a tornado picked up a dog-house, complete with dog inside, and dropped it upside down a few blocks away. The dog was dazed but not hurt.

A tornado in Lubbock, Texas, moved an empty fertilizer tank weighing 26,000 pounds about three quarters of a mile! Investigators couldn't tell whether it was airborne or if it rolled and tumbled—but either way, the wind was strong!

In 1920, Clair Westerman walked into her kitchen in Hobart, Oklahoma, after a tornado and was startled to see a two by four board sticking through the cabinet door where she kept her dishes. The cabinet door was still properly closed. Even weirder, not a single one of her dishes had been broken!

A Flint, Michigan, police officer had just stepped into his yard when he heard the "freight train roar" of a tornado. It slammed him against the side of his house. He was pinned there, his feet off the ground, and could only watch as a tree was twisted so violently that the individual fibers separated, like strands of a rope. The tornado passed, the man dropped to the ground, and the tree snapped back to its original shape—with straw and weeds sticking out of it, trapped when the tree closed back up.

Near Plainfield, Illinois, a tornado hit a tractor-trailer. The tractor ended up about 375 feet from the road without hitting ground once. The trailer was wrenched free of its hitch and was found in a field about 1,100 feet from the road. It bounced five times, leaving unmistakable scars on the ground, its cargo of scrap metal scattered.

✗   ✗   ✗   ✗   ✗   ✗

Why do tornadoes demolish one house, yet leave the one right next to it untouched? A large tornado funnel can have up to five or six smaller twisters, ranging from one to fifty yards across, spinning around inside it. When these suction vortices wander outside the boundaries of the main tornado, the results can get very freaky indeed.

A complex storm with several funnels lifted 67 freight cars off the tracks near Rothville, Missouri in May of 1971. Forty years earlier, in May, 1931, a tornado picked up five railroad coach cars and a 70-ton mail car from the tracks. Its coupling was still closed locked—impossible unless the train was lifted straight up. Another tornado blew 88 train cars off the track and stacked them three and four deep, like enormous toys.

Coal cars on a freight train were bounced up and down on the tracks by a tornado, then lifted from their wheels, spun around, and crashed down again. Amazingly, the train crew survived!

In the 1999 Oklahoma tornado, an 11-year-old boy and his mother were on the way home when the radio announced that a tornado was about to hit Chickasha. As the wind got bad, she pulled over at a viaduct. A lot of people were there already, but she found a hole and pushed her son into it, then lay down and held on to him to keep him from blowing away. When the wind lifted her, she told her son she loved him, then let go so he wouldn't be pulled upward with her. Rescue teams found her several blocks away; the tornado had killed her.

A tornado managed to lift a baseball dugout off its foundation and carried the heavy structure 150 yards.

After a 1995 tornado, debris was found spread over eight Oklahoma counties, spanning more than 100 miles. The items included a man's personalized jacket, transported nearly 20 miles from its source, and a flag from a golf course, carried 43 miles. The jacket was in perfect condition, the flag still attached to its plastic rod.

A Ford Bronco was picked up by a long-funneled tornado, carried over a church, and deposited 100 yards away.

After a 1995 tornado in Oklahoma, two pieces of paper about the same size and weight—that were picked up by the tornado from places over 10 miles apart—landed at the same spot! A much heavier textbook cover, from the same place as one of the pieces of paper, was found beside it.

In 1953, a tornado that hit Waco, Texas, buried some downtown streets under five feet of fallen bricks.

In Houston in 1993, a tornado ripped the garage out of a house but left the second story alone—a tornado-created car port!

Tornadoes can come in clusters, since the conditions that create them can cover a wide area. The largest number of tornadoes in recorded history was on April 3 and 4, 1974, when 148 twisters hit Alabama, Tennessee, Kentucky, Illinois, Indiana, Ohio, and Michigan, killing 315 people. Six of these tornadoes were F5—the highest measurement of intensity.

After a tornado, a Kansas family stepped outside to see the wreckage of their neighbors' home, then looked back and realized their own roof had been torn off!

In 1977, near Nashville, Tennessee, a woman and her son felt a tornado lift their house off the foundation. A second or two later, as if it had changed its mind, the tornado set it back down.

After an Oklahoma tornado, the bodies of two people who were together at home during a tornado were found two miles apart—as were pieces of their house.

One twister carried a refrigerator a quarter-mile, then dropped it on the roof of a bank.

Once a tornado in Broken Bow, Oklahoma, carried a motel sign 30 miles and dropped it in Arkansas! Canceled checks from Broken Bow (easy to trace because they are printed with names and addresses) were found 125 miles southeast.

In the 1999 Del City, Oklahoma, tornado, a man put his wife in the bathtub and covered her with pillows and blankets to protect her. Then, afraid the window would shatter and spray her with glass, he stood beside it, holding a pillow up to deflect the explosion. His wife tried to get him in the tub, under the cover of the bedding, but he refused. The tornado sucked him out through the window and he was killed.

Laundromat washing machines once rained from the sky when a tornado picked them up, then dropped them again. People could only watch, amazed as the huge machines dropped from the sky.

One inventive tornado carried a whole house, then dropped it so that it straddled a highway. In that same tornado, huge farm machinery rolled across fields like tumbleweed.

A Nebraska farmer was astonished to see a baby grand piano sitting in his field, where a tornado had set it down after carrying it 1,300 feet from its usual place in a living room.

In tornado winds, tin roofs can fly—becoming as lethal as giant buzz-saw blades. Steel I-beams sometimes seem to float like feathers. Almost everything you can imagine has been pulled into the air by a tornado. Fur coats and bathtubs have ended up in leafless tree tops. One man's car landed upside down in his neighbor's living room! After a tornado passed through her town, a woman found her mop *inside* a car down the street from her demolished house.

On May 3, 1999, with a tornado headed toward the Cracker Barrel Restaurant in Midwest City, Oklahoma, employee Mike Pederson hurried customers away from the front windows and into the back kitchen, then went out to keep watch. When he saw a massive wall of debris coming, he ran to warn everyone to get down. The tornado hit about fifteen seconds later. After it was over, a rental truck was in the middle of the dining room where he'd been standing. The kitchen was the only part of the restaurant that wasn't destroyed.

After the Great Bend, Indiana, tornado of 1915, a "rain of debris" littered farms as far as 80 miles northeast. Residents found strangers' receipts, checks, photographs, ledger sheets, money, clothing, shingles, pieces of books—and anything else you can imagine. A four-page letter from a young man to his girlfriend, promising her every-thing, was carried 70 miles. A necktie rack with 10 ties on it was carried 40 miles.

In this same tornado, mail was scattered for miles. Some people who found mail returned it to

Great Bend, and others sent it on to where it was supposed to go. This has to be one of the strangest forms of air mail!

The flying-debris record: A canceled check from Great Bend, Indiana, was found 305 miles away in a cornfield outside Palmyra, Nebraska. The longest-known-distance award for an object weighing over a pound goes to a sack of flour, carried 110 miles.

A tornado whirling down the 18th fairway of a golf course picked up a golfer and threw him 40 feet but did not hurt him.

A 1994 tornado sucked a man from the closet where he was huddled and threw him a thousand yards—that's the length of 10 football fields! He survived.

A Kansas woman was too close to a window during a tornado. The suction of the whirling winds pulled her out and dropped her 60 feet away. Next to her was found a record. The song recorded on it? "Stormy Weather."

✗　　✗　　✗　　✗　　✗　　✗

The "Great Tupelo Tornado" of 1936 demolished much of the small Mississippi town, killing 216 people. A rescue train that plowed through the wreckage to pick up the wounded had to leave town backward because it couldn't push all the way through the debris. The train, backing up all the way, dropped patients off at hospitals as far as Memphis, 100 miles away.

One woman who was trying to outrace a tornado was sucked out of her truck and thrown into a ditch. She said she was airborne, trying to run, but her feet wouldn't touch the ground. During her flight, she was joined by a live deer, flying through the air beside her.

Tornadoes struck Codell, Kansas, in 1916, 1917, and 1918—all three times on the same date, March 20.

A Pennsylvania couple had a wedding in 1985 that the guests will never forget. The wedding party was lined up in the hallway of the church, ready to go. Just as the organ started playing "Here Comes the Bride," a tornado struck. The windows exploded, glass rocketing across the room. The entire wedding party hit the floor, cut and bleeding.

Outside in the parking lot, a latecomer felt her car lift high into the air. It crashed down and she jumped out, unharmed. An hour later, the couple got married in their torn, bloody clothes. The guests were bandaged and battered, but they all survived.

On April 9, 1947, the night a tornado killed 181 people in Woodward, Oklahoma, the movie playing at the local theater was "Rage in Heaven."

After the infamous Woodward, Oklahoma, tornado, a four-year-old child's body was never identified. People think she might have been in a car passing through from out of state, and that her parents were killed and blown away, never to be found. The townspeople buried her in their graveyard, adopting her as their "fallen angel."

One tornado really made sparks fly in a small Midwestern town. A man sitting in a cafe noticed the barometer taking a sudden nose-dive. He went to the door and was shocked to see a blazing river of fire coming down the street. All of the flying scraps of tin, nails, and other metal objects were hitting the pavement so fast and hard that they threw off cascading plumes of sparks.

In 1957 a monstrous tornado hit the town of Leedy, Oklahoma, moving at only four mph. This gave the quick-witted and brave telephone operator time to ring all telephones, giving warning. Leedy was wiped off the face of the earth—not a building was left standing. But, thanks to the warning, only four people died.

In May, 1985, more than 100 people were playing bingo in an American Legion hall in Ohio when the tornado siren went off. They cowered beneath tables, listening to the roof peel off, smelling gas escaping from a broken pipe. Terrified of being blown up or blown away, they were amazed, when it was all over, to see their bingo cards still on the tables, every piece in place.

In 1994, a tornado hit Philadelphia a few days after the TV soap *All My Children* featured a tornado in Philadelphia.

A tornado outbreak on May 31, 1985 killed 19 people in Niles, Ohio. It could have been worse. A new—but still empty—nursing home was destroyed. The roller rink was demolished, too. One hour later, it would have been filled with 300 skaters.

In 1852 a tornado struck sparsely settled New Harmony, Indiana, killing 16 people. Seventy-three years later, in 1925, the famous "Tri-State Tornado" followed exactly the same path as the older one but this time, the populous region lost 695 people.

A year-old baby was unharmed in the Tupelo Tornado, although a church near his home was demolished. Maybe all the shouting and commotion influenced the music of Elvis Presley once he grew up!

After tornadoes roar across farming areas people often find chickens walking around naked—all of their feathers gone! These birds aren't hurt. They are clucking and crowing. There are lots of wild theories for this common sight, but the most likely cause is *flight molt*. When a fox grabs a chicken, the chicken protects itself by suddenly molting its feathers, leaving the fox with a mouthful of quills and fluff while it escapes. Probably, during a tornado, the frightened chicken sheds feathers until it runs out!

A chicken was found inside a rolled-up ball of barbed wire, still living, but plucked clean enough to put into a pot. How the barbed wire got rolled up around it—we can only guess.

When a tornado killed 45,000 migrating ducks, dead ducks fell from the sky as far as 40 miles northeast of the migratory bird refuge!

When tornadoes cross lakes or rivers, they suck water up and spew it out 100 feet or higher into the air. Sometimes a tornado will suck a small pond completely dry. In 1886, people could see the bottom of the Mississippi River as a tornado crossed it.

Waterspout tornadoes are just as capable of lifting heavy objects as their land-locked cousins. In Miami, a waterspout lifted a five-ton houseboat from the water.

Since ancient times, people have seen odd things falling from the sky in rainstorms: Fish, frogs, snails, dead ducks, clams, tadpoles, woodpeckers, and other birds, to name a few. Serious scientists scoffed at such tales and called them myths, until someone calculated that the lifting force of a waterspout could easily suck these animals from the air and water, carry them inland, and release them with the rain!

A dog and the tree it was tied to disappeared in a vicious tornado. Three days later, the scared, hungry dog was found in a field, still tied to a section of the shattered trunk.

In 1915, a tornado leveled a farm, killing two people. It demolished the barn but carried five horses a quarter-mile, setting them down unhurt, all still hitched to the same rail.

WEIRD TALES OF SURVIVAL

A twister whisked a two-year-old baby from his mother's arms. He later crawled out of a ditch, unharmed, but naked. The wind had torn his clothes off.

A Georgia couple was relieved when a tornado missed them by a mile. But about 45 minutes later, a friend rushed into their house and warned them that a second tornado was coming. They just had time to get their little girl out of bed and run to an interior hallway where they all crouched on the floor. Minutes later, that hallway was the only part of the house left standing.

In 1947, a man in Glacier, Texas, was swept from his basement and carried almost a quarter mile before the tornado gently plopped him head-first into a wild plum thicket.

On April 27, 1899, a woman and boy were picked up and carried more than two hundred feet high. As they soared over a church steeple, they were afraid they might get kicked by the white horse that was sailing along with them. They and the horse were carried for a mile—then all three landed, muddy but unharmed.

In the 1999 tornado that hit Oklahoma City and surrounding areas, two elderly people were in a tiny shelter, sitting side by side in folding chairs while the tornado raged. Part of the house collapsed and buried them alive. They were trapped for 24 long, frightening hours. A search and rescue dog that had been brought in from Nebraska finally found them!

In May, 1985, a Wheatland, Pennsylvania

woman heard hail beating on the roof. She jumped up from the dinner table to bring in baskets of flowers from the front porch, then couldn't close the door against the wind's force. Her husband helped, but even pushing together, the door snapped them backward, pinning them against the wall. Just then, razor-sharp pieces of a metal awning flew through the door and were driven into the dining table. Then the roof and second story rose up and disappeared. In seconds, the whole house was smashed and was blown away— except the hallway wall where they were pinned. Pink, powdery roof insulation packed their mouths and they could barely breathe, much less respond to shouting rescuers. Finally, one noticed the woman's hand, waving frantically above the door. Except for cuts and bruises, they were not hurt!

On May 25, 1896, 30 people were attending a funeral when a tornado struck. Terrified, they ran to lie down in a ditch until the winds subsided— and they all lived. Another man, less aware of tornado safety, watched from a window in his nearby house. The glass shattered and he was killed.

In Centerville, Illinois, where a one-room brick

schoolhouse once stood, there's a statue of a woman looking skyward, with her arms protectively around two children. The plaque reads: "In memory of Annie Louise Keller who saved sixteen children but sacrificed her own life when a tornado demolished Centerville School Building, April 19, 1927." Because she made sure that they all took cover, all sixteen of Annie's students survived, including the child found sheltered beneath her crushed body.

A twister once picked up a car with two passengers inside, carried it 100 feet, then set it down unscratched. The people were terrified, but all right.

An Oklahoma pioneer's daughter recalled her mother standing in an open doorway, watching a tornado pick up a neighbor's shed. The wind shrieked and she shouted, "Don't you drop that shed down on my garden!" The tornado dipped and lifted, then obediently let the shed fall outside the fence. The daughter remembers, "Not a bean in Mama's garden was disturbed."

Some people survive by bear-hugging something solid. One man lived through a tornado by lying on the ground and holding on to a car tire.

In an Ohio tornado, a woman saved her own life. Driving, she saw a tornado funnel coming right at her. She braked, jumped out and looked for a low spot or hole, but there was only flat cement. Desperate for something to cling to, she ran toward a sturdy signpost in a nearby gas station parking lot. The tornado gave her a boost, sucking her straight up, then spitting her out. In a split second, she was lying on the ground next to the post. She clutched it as the wind lifted her, then slapped her down over and over. A big tree and the gas station roof fell, but the sign protected her.

A Georgia rock climber saw a twister coming about 500 feet below him, and could only cling to the cliff face. He was battered by golf-ball–size hail, pieces of sheet metal, and other debris as the wind whipped him around like a piece of paper. Below him, his climbing partner tied the safety rope to a pine tree, then held on to the trunk. It was the only tree that survived the tornado.

A tornado once tossed a mobile home 125 feet without injuring a five-year-old girl asleep inside.

John and Naomi Bryan were living with their toddler in a mobile home next to her parents' farm. A tornado warning on TV sent them to her parents' storm cellar. They all waited underground, listening to the roar of the tornado as it went by to the north. Emerging, they decided it was safe and started home. Reaching their mobile home, they heard another roar.

John threw the car into reverse and turned back. An instant later he had to stand on the brakes as the roaring faded. The driveway he had just driven up was blocked by a huge, uprooted tree. The next morning they could see that the second tornado had knocked the tree down, jumped over their mobile home, and touched down behind it, almost certainly right over their heads just as they saw the downed tree. No one was hurt.

As a man clung to a telephone pole, a tornado plucked off both his shoes, one sock, and then his shirt buttons, but left him uninjured.

In Tennessee, a husband, wife, and three-year-old child took shelter in a pre-molded one-piece bathtub/shower unit. The house was totally destroyed, but the tub carried the family safely into the backyard.

✗   ✗   ✗   ✗   ✗   ✗

A man in a mobile home saw a tornado coming and grabbed hold of a mattress. He regained consciousness about 100 feet away, still atop his mattress and not seriously hurt.

In Wheatland, Pennsylvania, during May, 1985, Dave Kostka was umpiring a Little League baseball game. He saw a tornado coming. Thinking fast, he crammed spectators and players into the concrete dugout. With his seven-year-old niece, Christa, and Scott, a ten-year-old boy, Kostka started for his mother's house in his Blazer, trying to dodge the tornado. When it veered toward them, it lifted his Blazer, then dropped it. He pulled the kids out and got them into a ditch, then lay down on top of them. The tornado pried him from the ditch and smashed him into a wall, killing him instantly, but the kids managed to cling to the ground. Scott gripped Crista's ankle when the wind lifted her and held on until the fury passed. Kostka's brave actions didn't save him, but the people at the ballpark and Scott and Crista owe him their lives.

On April 14, 1986, an Arkansas couple in a campground heard a storm was coming and decided their motor home was not safe. They ran to a concrete block bathhouse and started to go inside, but at the last moment decided to lie down next to it instead. An instant later the tornado ripped into the bathhouse, and the only spot where the concrete blocks didn't fall was where the couple lay, terrified. Four people who had stayed near their campers were killed.

A twister blew a Philadelphia man through a second story window. He sailed about fifty feet to land in his neighbor's family room. He lived through the drop-in visit.

When a tornado struck his home, an infant rode the wind in his crib, was carried out onto the front lawn, and survived.

DANGEROUS MYTHS

Myth: The southwest corner of a building is the safest.

Truth: A 1966 study showed the corner closest to the approaching tornado is the most dangerous place to be—and most tornadoes come from the southwest. A house blown toward the northeast can shift off its foundations. The now unsupported southwest corner is likeliest to collapse.

Myth: An Osage Indian legend said tornadoes would never strike near the point where two rivers join.

Truth: Emporia, Kansas, sits "protected" between the Cottonwood and Neosho Rivers. On June 8, 1974 a tornado there killed six people and destroyed $20,000,000 worth of property. Another tornado did $6,000,000 worth of damage in Emporia on June 7, 1990. No site is protected.

Myth: You should open the windows in a tornado to keep the low pressure from exploding your house.

Truth: When a tornado hits, the winds often shove up under the eaves, pushing the roof upward—sometimes all the way off! With the roof gone, the walls fall outward, looking like the house has exploded. It hasn't. So, leave the windows alone and seek shelter!

HOW BAD WAS IT?

Meteorologists use the Fujita-Pearson Tornado Intensity Scale to measure tornado wind speeds:

F-0: (40–72 mph) Light damage: knocks over

chimneys and billboards, breaks branches off trees.

F-1: (73–112 mph) Moderate damage: peels surface off roofs, moves mobile homes, destroys attached garages.

F-2: (113–157 mph) Significant damage: snaps or uproots trees, tears off roofs, destroys mobile homes, pushes box cars over.

F-3: (158–206 mph) Severe damage: removes roof and walls from well-constructed homes, over-turns trains, lifts and tosses cars, uproots most trees in a forest.

F-4: (207–260 mph) Devastating damage: levels well-constructed homes; generates large airborne missiles, including cars.

F-5: (Greater than 261 mph) Incredible damage: lifts strong frame houses off foundations, sweeps them away, and dashes them to pieces; debarks trees; badly damages steel-reinforced concrete structures.

WHY, HOW, AND WHERE CAN IT HAPPEN?

One of the freakiest facts about tornadoes is that no one really knows what causes them. Scientists can list conditions needed for a tornado to form, but many times those same conditions don't produce tornadoes. If we can figure out what causes them, maybe someday we can stop torna-does before they start.

In the spring, cool, dry air from the north sweeps down over the warm, moist air coming up from the south. The cool air blows faster and at a higher alti-tude than the warm air. Because they are blowing in different directions, the air where they meet can start spinning, almost like a sideways tornado.

Warm air is less dense and lighter than cool air; that's why the air near the floor in your house is usually cooler than the air near the ceiling. On a much grander scale, when the warm, moist south-ern airflow rises, it forms a column that pushes rapidly upward through the cool, dry air from the north. The moisture in this air—as the air cools and contracts—condenses to form storm clouds. Usually, the result is thunderstorms and rain. But sometimes, the difference in wind speeds and directions might start the warm column rotating slowly. This alone won't make a tornado, but it is a good start. If the rising column tightens into a nar-row cylinder, it will spin faster and faster as it nar-rows—the same way a figure skater spins faster when she pulls her arms in. If that spinning col-umn of air works its way downward to touch the ground, we call it a tornado.

In the northern hemisphere, because of the prevailing wind patterns, most tornadoes spin counterclockwise and travel from southwest to northeast. Tornado winds swirl around the low pressure center of the funnel from 100 to 300 mph. The funnel can be a slim, graceful tube just 100 feet across, or a huge, roaring mile-wide wall of wind, dust, and debris. Every year, from 600 to 1,000 tornadoes touch down somewhere in the United States. They have occurred in every state, on every day of the year, at every hour of the day. But many will strike in the afternoon and early evening, in spring, along a 460-mile strip of land that includes Texas, Oklahoma, Kansas, and Nebraska. This area is called Tornado Alley. It gets about 300 tornadoes a year—about a third of the U.S. total. That's more than anywhere else on the planet.

The ten most deadly tornadoes in the United States:

1. The Tri–State Tornado (Missouri, Illinois, Indiana), March 18, 1925: 695 deaths and over 2,000 injured. This mile–wide killer slashed a 219–mile path through the three states.

2. Natchez, Mississippi, May 6, 1840: 317 deaths.

3. St. Louis/East St. Louis, Missouri Tornado, May 27, 1896: 255 deaths.

4. Tupelo, Mississippi, April 5, 1936: 216 deaths.

5. Gainesville, Georgia, April 6, 1936: 203 deaths.

6. Woodward, Oklahoma (Texas, Oklahoma, Kansas), April 9, 1947: 181 deaths.

7. Amite/Pine/Purvis (Amite, Louisiana/Purvis, Mississippi), April 24, 1908: 143 deaths.

8. New Richmond, Wisconsin, June 12, 1899: 117 deaths.

9. Flint, Michigan, June 8, 1953: 115 deaths.

10. A tie: Waco, Texas, May 11, 1953, and Goliad, Texas, May 18, 1902: 114 deaths each.

Many people die in tornadoes. Would you know what to do if you saw one coming? If there are disaster drills at your school, pay attention and take them seriously. A 500-yard-wide tornado severely damaged the high school and grade school in Pleasant Hill, Missouri, in 1977, but because of prior tornado drills, only one person died.

If you live in tornado country, you probably already know and understand what to do in a tornado. Instructions have been distributed in schools, given on radio and TV programs, even printed on paper grocery bags.

If you hear a TV or radio broadcaster talking about tornadoes, listen for these terms:

Tornado Watch: Conditions are right for a tornado to form.

Tornado Warning: A tornado has been sighted.

If you see severe weather approaching, react! If you are outside, at home or elsewhere, go inside. Take cover in any severe thunderstorm. Stay out of showrooms, stores, or businesses that have big windows.

Use a weather radio or battery-powered radio for weather updates if you can.

If there are thunderstorms, don't use a phone.

The wires could conduct an electrical charge that could injure or kill you.

If you are in your home or someone else's, and are told or can see that a tornado is coming, go to the storm cellar or to the basement if you can. Then get under the stairs or a heavy piece of furniture. If there is no basement, get inside a closet in the middle of the house. If there's no closet, go to an inside wall on the lowest floor. In any of these places: Kneel on the floor facing the wall, and cover your head with your hands and arms.

If you're at school, stay inside—but keep out of large rooms like gyms or auditoriums. They have wide roofs that could collapse.

If you are outside and can't make it to shelter, the idea is to get as low to the ground as you can. If there's a ditch or a low spot of any kind, lie down in it and cover your head with your hands and arms, and find something to hang on to.

If you are in a car, tell the driver to stop the car, and everyone should get out! There is little point in trying to outdrive a tornado. These powerful wind-funnels can go much faster than a car. And cars are often tipped or lifted, or panicked drivers cause crashes that kill passengers who might have survived the storm. One woman who survived a tornado by leaping from her car to hang on to a signpost walked back after the wind fell to find her purse on the front seat, cut to shreds by flying glass. The car behind her had been smashed into a pavilion, and the people in it were screaming. A van that had been nearby was upside-down on top of the gas pumps.

The best tornado advice is: Find shelter inside if you can, near a strong, interior wall or in a basement; outside, get low and find something to hang on to.

A NEW KIND OF HERO

During any kind of disaster, communications are cut off; long-distance phone capacity is often jammed. People outside the stricken area can't call to check on loved ones. Until recently, unless you were a ham radio operator, you could only wait in agonized limbo, watching grim and frightening TV reports. The Internet has changed all that. Online connections and chat rooms allow relatives to try to find someone who lives near their relatives to make the check-up call.

One of the authors is thankful to a man she knows only as "Shep," who contacted her mother in Oklahoma during the dreadful, anxious hours after the May 3, 1999, tornado, then relayed the welcomed news that she was all right. Throughout the night, Shep stayed online, taking phone numbers and checking on people. So Shep, whoever you are, thank you.

TERROR TECHS, WEATHER WIZARDS, AND DISASTER DOCTORS

Some people become so fascinated with tornadoes that they make a career—or a serious hobby—out of chasing and studying these amazing storms. They are far more careful than movie storm-chasers. They would never use dirt roads or drive across an open field. They keep several miles away from a tornado.

Tornado chasers might be National Weather Service employees, university professors, meteorologists with university degrees, students, or trained hobbyists. Their work will help meteorologists find out what happens before a tornado begins and why one thunderstorm spawns tornadoes while another—which looks the same—doesn't.

Trained, volunteer storm spotters alert local officials and the National Weather Service. They save many lives every year. There is a ham radio operators' spotter network called SKYWARN. To ask about storm spotter training, contact the National Weather Service or your county's Emergency Management office.

Remember: Storm chasing is NOT SAFE AND CAN KILL YOU—even if you are well-trained and have spent at least one storm season riding with an experienced chaser. Without training and experience, storm chasing is even more dangerous. If studying tornadoes interests you as a career, ask a school counselor about meteorology programs at colleges and universities.

FRIGHTFULLY FUNNY AND SERIOUSLY STRANGE

Meteorologist Charles A. Doswell III doesn't think we need a special name for tornadoes moving over water. If we're going to have waterspouts, then why not have special names for other tornadoes? He humorously suggests the following: Tornadoes over sand (sandspout), over asphalt (tarmacnado), over mobile homes (manufacturnado), and over eucalyptus trees (gumswirl).

One of the most famous cows in recent history is the unnamed, unfortunate bovine that sailed through the air in the movie *Twister*. Ever since her movie debut, she has provided entertainment for meteorologists and their students all over the country. Meteorologist Joseph D'Aleo came up with a new tornado intensity scale to replace the official Fujita Scale. He calls it the "MOOjita Scale."

M0 tornado—cows in an open field are spun around parallel to the wind flow and become mildly annoyed.

M1 tornado—cows are tipped over and "can't get up."

M2 tornado—cows begin rolling in the wind.

M3 tornado—cows tumble and bounce.

M4 tornado—cows are airborne.

M5 tornado—steak.

At the University of Michigan, atmospheric science professor Perry J. Samson and his daughters Karis and Carla rewrote the lyrics to Joni Mitchell's song "Both Sides Now"—in honor of *TWISTER*'s flying cow:

> *Flows of bovines in the air*
> *With udders flying everywhere*
> *So many milkshakes raining there*
> *I've looked at cows that way.*

But now they only blot the sun,
they spin and fall on everyone
I chased tornadoes but saw none
'Cause cows got in my way.
I've looked at cows
from both hides now
From udder down
and still somehow . . .
It's cows revolving
I recall.
I really don't know cows,
. . . at all.

chapter two

BLIZZARDS

imagine this . . .

It's 1887 and your family owns a big cattle ranch in the Panhandle region of Texas. Every night at supper, you sit around a big table that belonged to your mother's grandmother back in St. Louis. In the evening lantern light, your mother knits while your father goes over his account books, his face grim. You and your little brother play checkers or practice your reading and figures.

The cowboys who work for your father used to drive the herd north every year. For the cattle, the long journey overland to Wyoming ended with a long ride in a dark boxcar. The train journey took them to Chicago's stock yards, a major market center for beef. Once the cattle were delivered safely to the railhead, the cowboys turned around and rode all the way back to Texas, and your father collected a bank draft from the Chicago buyer.

Driving cattle north in herds has been a perfect arrangement for your father for years, but since winter before last, things have been changing. Because the money had been good for a while, more ranches were bought up in the

Panhandle—every year there have been more cattle on the land. To keep the herds from drifting southward to find winter shelter in canyons and valleys—and getting so mixed up their owners can't separate them come spring—the ranchers have strung miles-long barbed wire "drift fences." You and your father helped with the wire stringing. It seemed like the only answer to people farther south ending up with your cattle.

And the drift fences worked all right until two winters ago. In 1885 there was a series of ugly, freezing cold blizzards that swept over the southern plains. While you shivered around the fireplace with your family and sipped coffee and hot cider trying to stay warm, the cattle drifted south, trying to escape the fierce weather. But the fences stopped them. That year, many cows had been trapped against the barbed wire, unable to go any farther. They huddled against each other along the fence lines, and many froze to death.

No one thought the bad winter could repeat itself, so they counted up their losses and left the drift fences alone. But the winter of 1886 was no better, and this winter is the worst of all.

Riding with your father you've seen bunches of miserable cattle as much as 400 yards wide. They can't stay warm against the battering storms that seem to go on endlessly and you know most will smother or freeze if the weather stays as bad as it has been. They are dying in icy creek beds and snow-choked gullies. The wolves and coyotes are fat and sleek, circling the milling cows.

All winter you have been helping your father and the ranch hands try to get feed and water to at least some of the dying cows.

Last year, in January 1886, you followed your father from one end of the ranch to the other, riding in the bitter cold, adding up the number of carcasses—and you know that this year is worse.

On January 28, 1887, a blizzard rampages across the plains for three days, leaving millions of dead cattle behind. Three of your father's hired hands, trying to break the crusted snow so the cattle can find winter grass, freeze to death, caught out in a storm. Your mother and little brothers stay inside the house while you help your father and the other cowboys bury their friends in the icy ground. They build fires to soften the frozen earth enough to dig the graves.

A neighbor's cabin is buried beneath drifting snow. You notice, riding past, and try to dig them out. The job is too big and you start home to get help. Halfway there, the wind kicks up. In the last mile, the snow is blowing so thick that you cannot see the ranch in the distance anymore. Teeth chattering, your shoulders humped up against the cutting wind, you can only give your mare her head and hope that her instincts will find the barn.

It seems like an eternity, but the mare finally stops, tossing her head. You open your wind-burned eyes and cry out in relief. She has halted only because the barn door is shut. Stiff-legged and shivering, you slide out of the saddle.

It takes four cowboys, you and your father and five hours of digging the next morning to get the neighbors' front door open. No one has died, but they are all bluish with cold. They accept your mother's gifts of food and coffee and set about gathering firewood for the next storm.

That night your father closes his account book and shakes his head. He says he has given up. Your mother begins to weep quietly as he explains you will be moving to St. Louis where he will try to find work. The cruel winters have changed your life forever.

Months later, following the wagon road north, you pass piles of cow bones, and looking at them, you shiver, even though the day is warm.

After snow-melt in the spring of 1887, a cowboy found a dead cow high up in a tree, caught in the branches. It had probably been foraging for buried leaves while standing on top of a high snow drift during the terrible blizzard that winter.

In February, 1899, ice and snow drifted downstream in the Mississippi River—floating south from the blizzard-stifled Midwest and west. These ice floes blocked the Mississippi River at New Orleans, then floated into the Gulf of Mexico to melt. This happened in 1784, too, during another fierce winter.

The largest snowflakes on record fell January 28, 1878 over an area of several square miles in Montana. Witnesses said they were "larger than milk pans." When measured, the huge snowflakes were found to be 15 inches across and eight inches thick!!

During the February 6, 1978, New England blizzard, 10-year-old Peter Gosselin was last seen playing in huge snow banks near his home. Three thousand people searched for him for the next three weeks. On February 27, a mailman noticed a mitten protruding from a snow mound just a few feet from the boy's front door—and discovered Peter's body.

In Great Falls, Montana in 1887, 5,000 blizzard-starved steers invaded the town. They ate everything they could find, including paper and trash.

In 1888, a blizzard paralyzed the entire Northeast, from Maryland to Maine. Troy, New York, got a whopping 55 inches of snow. Many towns didn't even try to clear their streets. They shoveled their sidewalks, dumping snow into the middle of the streets, then dug tunnels through the mounds so pedestrians could cross!

In the town of Medora, North Dakota, hundreds of milling cattle roamed the streets during the 1887 blizzards. Residents nailed boards over their windows to prevent the starving cows from breaking them in their desperate search for food. The cattle ate tarpaper they pulled from the walls of shacks. It poisoned them, and they sickened and died.

After a blizzard, when the sky clears, temperatures often plunge. A phenomenon called "diamond dust" happens in extremely cold weather. If it is cold enough, ice crystals can condense directly from the air and sift earthward from an otherwise clear sky.

The most dangerous blizzards on earth are in the Antarctic, where winds up to 90 miles an hour sweep knife-sharp ice particles over the hard-packed snow surface.

New York is the snowiest state in the United States. Buffalo, New York, gets more snow than any other large city (1,109.8 inches in the seventies).

Modern blizzards don't kill as many people or animals because we now have much better homes and heating. But in January, 1967, a blizzard ravaged Chicago for 29 hours. Almost 60 people died during the storm and afterward—due to heart attacks as people tried to shovel the massive snowfall away from their doors and driveways.

After a 1979 Chicago blizzard that stalled all transportation, including garbage trucks, there were problems we don't usually associate with blizzards. Because of the buildup of garbage, rats multiplied dramatically and were a problem for a long time afterward!

The 1886 and 1887 blizzards were called the "Big Die-Up." On one Texas ranch, cowboys had rounded up 10,000 calves in 1886. After that awful winter, they found only 100 yearlings that had survived.

The 1886 blizzard killed eighty percent of the cattle in the state of Kansas.

Over 400 people died in the blizzard of 1888, 200 of them in New York City alone. There were many tragic stories. Factory workers and farmers collapsed on their doorsteps. The wind was so strong that it knocked over grown men on the sidewalks as they walked to work! Blinded by ice and snow, children froze to death only a few yards from their homes.

The 1888 blizzard brought all traffic to a halt. Even the elevated trains in New York City had to stop, and some passengers were stranded between stations. Gypsies offered ladders so the passengers could get down from the high tracks—for a fee of a dollar a person. That was a lot of money in 1888!

Outside the cities, marooned train passengers rummaged through baggage cars for food, bought supplies from local farmers, and paid a dollar for sandwiches which should have cost a nickel back then. They broke up seats and other furnishings in the train and started fires to keep warm!

During the 1888 blizzard, the Brooklyn Bridge was the only way in and out of New York City. All the ferry crossings were closed because of ice on the water. City officials saw pedestrians clinging to the bridge rail and pulling themselves hand-over-hand against the raging gale, so they closed access to the bridge.

The next morning, floes of ice and snow had wedged together, forming an ice bridge just south of the man-made one. Some reckless citizens crossed it. But when the tide went out later, the ice broke up. Over 100 people were trapped on the floes and were barely able to escape!

Most theaters in New York City were closed down by the 1888 blizzard. But one play drew about 100 dedicated patrons to Daly's Theater in time to catch a Shakespeare play. The title? *A Midsummer Night's Dream.*

The New York City street cleaners had their share of hard work during and after the blizzard of 1888. The snow was packed into such hardened drifts that they had to use axes and picks to clear the streets!

One good thing came out of the 1888 New York blizzard. Legislators decided that they would never again have their telegraph and telephone lines broken down from snow and wind. They began the long, hard task of putting all the cables underground as soon as work could be begun.

WEIRD TALES OF SURVIVAL

Fifteen-year-old O. W. Meier and his brothers, twelve and eight, barely got home from school during an 1888 blizzard in Nebraska. He recalled, "My brothers and I could not walk through the deep snow in the road, so we took off down the rows of corn stalks to keep from losing ourselves till we reached our pasture fence. Walter was too short to wade the deep snow in the field, so Henry and I dragged him over the top. For nearly a mile we followed the fence till we reached the corral and pens. In the howling storm, we could hear the pigs squeal as they were freezing in the mud and snow. Sister Ida had opened the gate and let the cows in from the field to the sheds, just as the cold wind struck and froze her skirts stiff around her like hoops. The barn and stables were drifted over when we reached there. The roaring wind and stifling snow blinded us so that we had to feel through the yard to the door of our house. The lamp was lighted. Mother was walking the floor, wringing her hands and calling for her boys. Pa was shaking the ice and snow from his coat and boots. He had gone out to meet us but was forced back by the storm.

"The next morning we walked out upon the hard deep drifts and shoveled a way through to the barn where we found our cows and horses alive on top of the snow that had drifted into their stalls, but a lot of our hogs were frozen stiff in mud, ice and snow. The road we came over on our way home was strewn with frozen quails and rabbits, dead."

It was truly an awful night on the open plains. Both teachers and school children died in the storm.

In May 1996, there was a blizzard atop Mount Everest. Lene Gammelgaard had just reached the summit—making her the first Scandinavian woman to conquer the world's highest mountain. The next day she was faced with surviving the mountain's deadliest disaster. The catastrophic blizzard killed eight climbers, including Scott Fischer, the expedition leader, but Lene Gammelgaard managed to descend to safety.

On February 6, 1978, a blizzard caused a 5,000-vehicle traffic jam in Providence, Rhode Island. One woman about to give birth was trapped in her car. Her two companions recruited two strangers. The four men carried her, over their heads, several blocks through drifts and biting winds to the hospital, where her baby was born safely!

HOW BAD WAS IT: SCALES AND MEASURES

Snowfall record for a single storm: February, 1959, at California's Mount Shasta Ski Bowl—189 inches.

Record snowfall for a single month: 1911, Tamarack, California—390 inches.

Record snowfall for a twelve-month period: February 19, 1971 to February 18, 1972, Ranier Paradise Ranger Station in Washington State—1,224.5 inches.

Record snowfall for a 24-hour period: April 14 and 15, 1921 at Silver Lake, Colorado—75.8 inches.

The record for the deepest snow was set in March of 1911 in Tamarack, California: 451 inches. That's almost four stories high.

Cold winters sometimes mean more blizzards than usual:

On January 23, 1971, Prospect Creek Camp in Alaska recorded minus 79.8 degrees! That's the lowest temperature in U.S. weather history. The lowest recorded American temperature outside Alaska is minus 69.7 F, recorded on January 20, 1954 at Rogers Pass, Montana. That is cold enough to freeze your lungs as you breathe.

Snow sometimes falls on palm trees! The most southerly trace of snow in American weather history was January 19, 1977, at Homestead, Florida—nearly the southernmost point on the USA mainland.

In January, 1985, a record snowstorm hit western and south central Texas. The palm trees of San Antonio were blanketed with up to thirteen and a half inches of snow. This was more snow from one storm than the area usually got in a whole winter.

The "Blizzard of 1932" hit Los Angeles, bringing with it a full two inches of snow. This wouldn't have impressed anyone from real snow country, but it shocked southern Californians.

WHY, HOW, AND WHERE CAN IT HAPPEN?

Much of the United States is blizzard-prone. During the months of January, February, and March of each year, blizzards often stop our cities cold. Though we have learned a lot about how to avoid major disruptions and minimize deaths and injuries, blizzards are still a major problem.

A blizzard is a storm system with winds of at least 35 mph, temperatures below 20 degrees F, and ground visibility less than a quarter mile. It doesn't have to be snowing to be a blizzard. If the winds stir up enough old snow to limit visibility it's a ground blizzard.

A *whiteout* is an extreme blizzard condition when blowing or falling snow is thick enough to make the sky, the air, and the ground look white. People caught in a whiteout can get completely lost in minutes, and sometimes freeze to death or get hurt because they can't find their way to shelter.

Meteorologists have given names to winter storms because of where they come from and how they develop. One of these is probably the kind of storm your area gets most often.

Nor'Easters: The strength of these storms is matched only by hurricanes. They form near the populous, usually warm, Atlantic coast, then sweep northward. As a Nor'easter progresses, the effects of colder air occur. Rain changes to freezing rain, sleet, and finally snowfall. At the same time, cities near the Great Lakes can suffer from lake-effect snows—strong west-northwest winds in the wake of Nor'Easters pull moisture off the lakes dumping snow on the whole region. East coast residents dread the high winds, heavy precipitation (rain, ice, and snow), and the potential for coastal flooding that accompany Nor'Easters.

Alberta Clipper: These storms form on the lee side of the Canadian Rockies in the province of Alberta. The friction from the mountains causes air flow to break up into eddies and circulations that— with the right conditions—form surface low-pressure centers. Once the storm is formed, it often moves fast, roaring into the Great Lakes and New England. Clippers bring cold air and wind. As they move, cold air is "pulled" from northern Canada into the Great Lakes and Ohio Valley. This cold air—

combined with strong winds from a steep pressure gradient—helps Chicago live up to its windy and chilly wintertime reputation. Alberta Clippers are usually dry storms, bringing only a dusting of snow. But when they pick up moisture from the Great Lakes, they can produce formidable blizzards.

Texas Panhandler: When cold air flowing down the front range of the Rockies hits warm air and moisture from the Gulf of Mexico, the flat land of the Texas Panhandle becomes the mixing zone. Jet-stream disturbances rotating over this mixing zone create lift, which can intensify surface low pressure into a significant winter storm. Texas Panhandlers move slowly east and often produce plenty of snow north of the warm front.

Siberian Express: Not actually a storm, a Siberian Express is an arctic air mass behind a fast-moving cold front. These can come from near the North Pole—and sometimes even from Siberia. Many record-breaking low temperatures can be credited to a Siberian Express. As the arctic front pushes through, heavy, dense, and guided into the central and eastern U.S. by the mountain ranges, there can be an hour or less of heavy precipitation that races along just ahead of the front. Sweeping southward, the front brings winds up to 50 to 60 miles an hour, and since the air is so cold, life-threatening wind chill factors.

Chattanooga Choo-Choo: Forming in the Ohio Valley, Chattanooga Choo-Choos are storms that intensify over eastern Tennessee. They usually form along the western slope of the Appalachians when a cold front—the air dense and heavy—struggles to clear the mountains.

As they strengthen, Choo-Choos often bring in cold, moist Great Lakes airflows which usually add sleet and snow. They also move slowly northeast, producing 24 to 36 hours of constant snow over much of the Appalachians and the Ohio Valley. The lower elevations of the Piedmonts often get rain from Choo-Choos, since the cold air doesn't usually make it into that region. Since Chattanooga Choo-Choos move slowly, the upper-level processes that help their development can "outrun" them, producing a coastal storm that can become a Nor'easter. When the storm types join, the coast can get a double whammy.

February 27, 1717: The Great Snow of 1717 was a series of four storms that dumped up to five feet of snow on some parts of New England. The snowfall starved about 95% of New England's deer population by burying the grass and brush they fed upon.

December 26, 1778: The Hessian Storm was named for nine German mercenaries who froze at their posts in Newport, Rhode Island. It hit southern New England, and more than 50 people were reported frozen to death in the 18-inch snowfall and sub-zero temperatures. The winds wrecked many ships, including the American brig *General Arnold*, killing nearly 100 people off Plymouth, Massachusetts. Twenty-eight vessels were beached on Staten Island by the gale.

January 14–15, 1831: This was the worst snowstorm on record before 1888. Several inches of snow fell as far south as Georgia and as far west as the Ohio Valley. Gettysburg, Pennsylvania, recorded 30 inches. Pittsburgh had 22 inches.

January 18–19, 1857: The Great Cold Storm

brought heavy snow, below freezing temperatures, and gale-force winds. Temperatures were –40° F at Watertown, New York. In Jacksonville, Florida, the temperatures were as low as 16° F. Twelve-foot-high snow banks blocked railroad tracks around New York City. Washington, D.C. got nearly two feet of fresh snow, and Athens, Georgia, had eight inches.

January 12, 1888: The First Great Blizzard of 1888 hit the western states. Following a warm, almost springlike morning, the storm swept down out of the Dakotas to Texas. Many people were killed, including children and settlers caught far from shelter. In the northeast, the storm hit hard too, with New York City buried in snow.

February 1, 1899: The temperature fell to 61 degrees below zero in Montana while the "Great Eastern Blizzard" left a blanket of snow from Georgia to New Hampshire. The state of Virginia had snowfall totals averaging 30 to 40 inches.

January 22, 1922: The Knickerbocker Storm dumped 28 inches of snow on Washington, D.C., getting its name when the roof of the Knickerbocker

Theater collapsed under the weight of the snow, killing 100 moviegoers.

November 11, 1940: The Armistice Day Storm howled over the Great Lakes and the Upper Midwest. Muskegon, Michigan, recorded winds of 67 mph. Ships and boats on Lake Superior and Lake Michigan were wrecked; 59 sailors died. Iowa got 17 inches of snow. Forty-nine people in Minnesota died because of the storm.

March 15, 1941: One of the worst blizzards in modern times swept across the northern plains on a Saturday night, catching people out on the town for the evening. In North Dakota, 39 people died in the storm; 32 succumbed in Minnesota. Grand Forks, North Dakota, measured 85 mph winds, and Duluth, Minnesota, clocked wind speeds up to 75 mph.

December 26, 1947: New York City's 27-inch snowfall covered the city in 24 hours. The death toll from the storm was 27. It cost $8 million to remove the snow from streets and building roofs.

January 2, 1949: This savage series of storms lasted seven weeks on the Great Plains. During breaks in the heavy snowfall, winds gusting to 80 mph formed massive drifts from the fine, powdery snow. It filled deep gullies and small valleys! Temperatures got as low as -50° F. Two hundred people died from various storm-related causes. Farm animals died by the thousands on the open range: around 125,000 sheep and 25,000 cattle.

January 10, 1975: A "100-year storm" blew into Minnesota with a windchill factor as low as -80° F. As much as two feet of snow fell. There were 35 storm-related fatalities.

February 6–7, 1978: The biggest blizzard in southern New England's modern history struck Boston, following an earlier storm that had already left up to two feet of snow. As new snow piled on top of the old, two tractor-trailers jackknifed on Route 128 and blocked the road. Thousands of people had to abandon their cars; many sought shelter in churches. For the first time in 106 years, the Boston *Globe* newspaper wasn't printed. Traffic was at a standstill for nearly five days, as more than 27 inches of new snow fell on Boston.

Storm of the Century, March, 1993: This

Nor'easter produced record low pressures, high wind speeds, freezing temperatures and snowfall amounts. It left a destructive and paralyzing path of heavy snow throughout the southeast. Areas that never get more than 6 to 8 inches of snow in a year got 20 inches from this storm. New York City got 15 inches of snow. Areas in Pennsylvania and New Jersey had close to 20 inches.

Seventy record lows were set on March 14, with an additional 75 that following morning. About 270 people died of storm-related causes. About 25% of the United States' flights for two days were canceled and property damage estimates were over $3 billion. Twenty-six states were affected, impacting the lives of nearly 100 million people, approximately half the population of the USA.

Winter Storm Watches and Warnings

An announcement that a winter storm watch is in effect means severe winter weather may affect your area. A storm warning indicates that severe winter weather is definitely on the way. A blizzard warning means that large amounts of falling or blowing snow and sustained winds of at least 35 miles per hour are expected.

If you live in a place where snowstorms are frequent in the winter, you are at risk for a blizzard-attack! Listen to local forecasts and pay attention to severe weather warnings in your area. You can suggest to your parents that being prepared is being smart. Here are some things to ask them to consider:

- Keeping enough heating fuel on hand.
- Adding insulation to your house.
- Buying safe, effective emergency heating equipment.
- Putting together a good disaster kit.

EVERY GOOD DISASTER KIT INCLUDES:

- Flashlight and extra batteries.
- Portable, battery-operated radio and extra batteries.
- A good first-aid kit.
- One-week food supply that needs no refrigeration or cooking.
- A nonelectric can opener.
- A week's supply of any prescription medications needed by anyone in your family.
- Blankets and sleeping bags and adequate coats.
- Fire extinguisher (A–B–C type).

Many families have an Emergency Plan. They decide where they will meet if an emergency strikes while they are scattered at work, at school, or elsewhere. You can also appoint an out-of-state relative—someone who lives far enough away to be unaffected by any local disaster—to act as "message central" for your family. Make sure everyone knows the name, address, and phone number of the contact person.

Then, if a blizzard or some other disaster strikes, you and the rest of your family will be able to communicate.

Watch Out for Wind Chill

Wind chill is how cold it *feels* when the effects of temperature and wind speed are combined. A strong wind on a cold day can affect your body as if the temperature were about 35 degrees colder!

Blizzard Dress Code

In severe cold weather, dress in layers. Wear a hat that covers your ears. Mittens are warmer than gloves. Wear insulated boots. If the air is extremely cold, cover your mouth with a scarf or ski mask—or even your hand—to protect your lungs from the freeze. In hard-winter areas, it's a good idea to carry blankets in your car trunk.

If you are stranded in a car, stay inside it. Use the heater about ten minutes every hour, and crack a downwind window to prevent carbon-monoxide poisoning while the engine is on. Conserve gasoline, and don't run the battery down. Use whatever extra clothes, trunk-blankets, or even newspapers you have to cover yourself and conserve body heat. If you are with other people, huddle together.

Don't try to walk to safety until the worst of the storm passes. Set out on foot *only* if you can see a building that would provide shelter.

TERROR TECHS, WEATHER WIZARDS, AND DISASTER DOCTORS

A blizzard is very cold, fast moving water. Scientists studying blizzards have been working on ways to stop it, store it, and use it the following years when the crops and livestock need water.

Finding ways to control where and how snow drifts was the job of the USDA Forest Service's Rocky Mountain Research Station in Laramie, Wyoming. These researchers (two of them were nicknamed "Snowman" and "Blizzard Wizard") spent many winters building scale models of snow pits, wind shelters, and snow fences. Then, when a blizzard hit, they would wait to see where the snow had piled up.

The researchers wanted to learn how big a snow fence would keep drifts out of the calving barn and corrals, and how far blowing snow has to go before it evaporates. And it will evaporate, even in below freezing temperatures! They experimented with leaving corn stalks from one year's crop standing in the fields to trap snow—and water— for the following year's crop and with digging pits to trap snow to water livestock six months later in the heat of summer. Because of the research of Snowman, BlizWiz, and their co-workers, we are finding ways to make blizzards useful!

Blizzards create other jobs, too. The highly trained Nordic Search & Rescue Team has helped with wandering kids, lost hunters, urban disasters, mud slides, avalanches, ski lift evacuations, downed aircraft, snowbound shepherds—and more—throughout California and Nevada. Most of their calls are to help people lost in the rugged wilderness of the Sierra Nevada. Most of these searches and rescues are at night—or in blizzards. Many states have similar rescue teams.

FRIGHTFULLY FUNNY AND SERIOUSLY STRANGE

In 1880, a Vermont farm boy named Wilson Alwyn Bentley saw a snowflake through his mother's new microscope, and fell in love. He tried to draw snowflakes at first, then gave up, unable to capture their delicate and complex beauty. Then he talked his father into buying a camera that could take pictures through a microscope. As strange as it might sound, he devoted his life to snowflakes —he photographed around 4,500 of them!

The Great Snow of 1717 killed 1,100 sheep on a farm on Fisher's Island, in Long Island Sound. Twenty-eight days after the storm, two sheep were dug out of a 16-foot-high snowdrift. They had survived by eating the wool of their frozen companions.

To thaw the frozen pipes in his house in Farmingville, New York, a man backed his car up against an open window and turned on the engine—hoping the exhaust would warm the basement. Shortly afterward, the man, his wife, and their three children were taken to the hospital to be emergency-treated for carbon monoxide poisoning.

In blizzard season, one Ohio man diagnosed his car's problem as a frozen fuel line and decided to thaw it by running warm gasoline through it. He tried to heat a two-gallon can of gasoline on a gas stove! The explosion caused second- and third-degree burns on his face and head.

After a blizzard, one farmer had to cut a hole in his barn roof to milk his cows. The snow was drifted so deep against the doors it was the only way in!

chapter three

FLOOD

imagine this . . .

It is 1927 and your family lives on a cotton farm in Mississippi. Behind the house, rising like a steep grassy hill, is the slope of the levee—a thirty-foot-high mound of dirt that runs from hundreds of miles north of your house to hundreds of miles south of it. It was built over the last century—each town maintaining the section close by, long stretches of it kept up by farmers like your father.

If you walk up the slope to the top, you can see down the other side of the levee, all the way to the Mississippi River. On most days, the river course is a half mile away behind a thick line of trees.

But this year, it has been raining off and on for two months—hard, heavy rains. And the river has been rising. Radio programs have been talking about the flooding up north along the Missouri River. When you walk to the top of the levee, you see muddy brown water lapping at the base of the slope. The trees that once lined the river a half mile distant are nearly under water now.

A week later, the rushing dark river is still rising. It's only a yard or two down the slope on the other side of the levee. The distant treetops have disappeared and every day the water climbs higher. When you go back down the slope to your family's back porch, you glance over your shoulder at the thirty-foot-high levee and imagine what it would be like if the brown water climbing up the other side suddenly began to seep through, cutting a hole in the dirt and grass, thundering downward like a mud-colored waterfall.

You know it could happen. You have heard your parents talking about it late at night. Everyone is worried now. That kind of terrifying hole in the dirt levee is called a crevasse and everyone is watching the slope for signs of water seeping through. Sitting in the house waiting for the terrible cry of "crevasse!" to be shouted out, you can barely eat supper some nights. And it is still raining.

Day after day passes and one morning you waken to a yard full of water. It creeps along the ground. Even though your own levee has not yet broken, someone's has. From somewhere to the north, the escaped water is flowing over the land. It fills the low places first, the bayous and the lowlands, but then it creeps higher.

After a week, the porch steps are covered by muddy water. Then it rises to the front door. You and your friends think it is fun at first. You build rafts and use your father's small boat to row to town for groceries.

Then, one morning, your mother announces that you are going to move all your furniture to the second floor of the house and other belongings into the attic. You help, working hard alongside the rest of your family.

The water is rising faster now. By nightfall, the water is so high that you can't use your front door anymore. It is under water. You climb, with your parents, into your father's little boat and paddle to the top of the levee. There is high water on both sides now. In fact, it is beginning to trickle over the top of the levee.

You go to bed that night on the levee, beneath a piece of scrap canvas stretched between stakes driven into the ground. You listen and listen to the sound of rain hitting the cloth from the other side, waiting for the roar that will mean the levee beneath you is collapsing. . . .

The scene above happened in thousands of places during the Great Mississippi Flood of 1927. It was one of the worst natural disasters ever to happen in the United States. Many people took refuge on the levees. More than a thousand people were killed and 900,000 more lost their homes.

Strange but true: The levees that saved people might also have made the flood worse because they were built in a straighter line than the natural river bed had been; reducing the wide natural curves made the rain-swollen river run faster, its current stronger. But when people rebuilt the levees after the 1927 flood, they straightened out the river even more.

Sixty-six years later, in 1993, the Mississippi went on another rampage. That summer, a long rainy season in the Midwest brought three times the normal amount of rain. It saturated the ground, then ran into creeks and rivers—which all connected to the mighty Mississippi. The Mississippi rose and people piled sandbags on top of the levees, but the water finally destroyed many of them. In places the Mississippi River was seven miles wide!

At the peak of the flood, a land area the size of the state of Indiana was under water. Hundreds of thousands of acres of farm land were destroyed. Water rushing from a levee break buried one farm beneath nearly a million tons of sand!

THE JOHNSTOWN FLOOD

In May of 1889, the streets of Johnstown, Pennsylvania, were full of water—but no one was worried. The town flooded every year. People just began moving their household goods upstairs as always, annoyed at having to do it once again. They fully expected to have to bring everything back downstairs in a month or so.

Fourteen miles away, upstream, people were frantically trying to keep the South Fork dam from breaking. When they failed, a wall of water and debris a half mile wide and 40 feet high roared into Johnstown with all the force of Niagara Falls. Survivors said it looked like a moving hill, coming straight at them, littered with broken rooftops, shattered trees and pieces of walls and furniture! As the flood smashed its way through Johnstown, it picked up whole houses, barns, animals, people—everything in its path. The flood killed 2,209 people, including 99 entire families and 396 young children.

When the huge surge of water rushed past the Pennsylvania Railroad Company's Stone Bridge, a lot of the debris was piled against it. It made a colossal stack of twisted garbage forty feet high, covering thirty acres. Hundreds of people who had been swept along crawled desperately up the wreckage and managed to run to higher ground. But around 80 people remained trapped and were killed when the heap caught fire later that night.

It took fifty undertakers to bury the victims of the Johnstown flood. Bodies were still being discovered seventeen years later.

THE BIG THOMPSON FLOOD

On Saturday, July 31, 1976, Coloradoans were celebrating their centennial. The Big Thompson Canyon was crowded with happy campers. That evening, it began to rain. Then it poured. Between 6:30 and 11:00 p.m., over a foot of rain fell on the western end of the canyon. Amazingly, the water level in the Big Thompson River rose nineteen feet! A wall of churning water crashed and thundered down the canyon, going faster than 20 feet per second between the steep canyon walls. No one could outrun such swift water. It was even impossible to out-drive it! The raging river destroyed 418 homes and 52 businesses and killed 145 people.

Floods do strange things. Over 2,800 homes were destroyed by the 1972 Rapid City flood, and one woman watched her house float away as she escaped to higher ground. Later, she found her house a block down the street, with almost nothing damaged. Even the books were still in the bookcase.

After the same flood, another woman was seen calmly going through the linen closet of one of her upstairs rooms, which had come to rest, all in one piece, in the middle of a golf course.

During a 1964 Oregon flood, the Klammath River swept many of Lena McCovey's belongings away, including a bottle of pills with her name on it. Her sister, who lived 200 miles downstream in Coos Bay, Oregon, found the bottle.

Sometimes flood waters carry their victims a long way before they are found. The body of a Johnstown Flood victim was found in Steubenville, Ohio, over a hundred miles away, and sent back to Johnstown for burial.

Every year in America, several people die because they insist on crossing flooded rivers—even if the authorities have put up barricades to stop them. In January, 1998, during a Louisiana flood, a man drove around the barricades and into the swift water of a flood. His car stalled, and when he got out and tried to walk back to the barricade, the water knocked him down and he drowned.

In March of the same year, officials in Missouri were still milling around, working at putting up flood barricades at a low-water crossing when a woman drove up, wheeled right past them and drove into the water. Her pickup was swept away.

Flash floods can happen so suddenly that people don't have any time to prepare. A dry gully can go from dusty to disastrous in just a minute or two—sometimes within seconds in a severe enough rainstorm. Empty gullies all over the southwest—and elsewhere—can fill with ten or more feet of raging water. Rock climbers in Arizona learned this the hard way in 1997. Several people were trapped and drowned.

One of the freakiest things about floods is the

awesome power of moving water. Floods can kill people who don't realize how powerful even shallow water can be. Just six inches of swiftly moving water can knock you off your feet. Even the heaviest cars can be swept away in two feet of racing flood water!

After an Oregon flood, an insurance adjuster interviewed an elderly man who lived in a log cabin. He asked the man how high the water had gotten, and the man said, "forty-six inches." Then he explained that he knew his floor was forty-seven inches off the ground and the water had come within an inch of it! Sometimes people know the depth of water in a flood because they know how high their roof peak is.

Moving water has enough force to change the course of rivers forever, gouging out new curves and eroding away old ones. Often, after flood waters recede, the flooded river runs in a new course.

An Oregon man told an insurance adjuster that a flood had carried a "car-sized" boulder away from his front yard. When the adjuster drove back to the freeway, he passed a house with a big car-sized hole through the middle he could see right through. It was clear where the old man's missing boulder had gone!

Floods sometimes bury whole houses in mud and debris. Where does the mud come from? Upstream. In 1993, in California, the Santa Margarita River flooded and scoured out a whole new river bottom—several feet lower than the old one had been.

Floods don't respect holidays! On New Year's Day, 1934, heavy rain that had started a few days earlier led to flooding in the Los Angeles Basin area of California. Forty-five people were killed by walls of water and debris sweeping in ten-foot-high waves through some of the local canyons.

Living by a river is terrible at flood time. Imagine living *in* one! In a normal fresh water stream, about 45% of the young fish die every year. German scientists say that during floods, up to twice that percentage of some species die. Many of them are carried out to sea. Others starve. They are too busy fighting the currents to look for food—or their food is washed away!

The 1993 flood of the Mississippi dumped a ten-mile-wide current of fresh water into the Gulf of Mexico. This intrusion of fresh water flowed around the tip of Florida and into the Atlantic Ocean. Salt water fish were forced farther out to sea until the salt and fresh waters mixed. Some were killed.

In 1995, heavy rain in Thailand flooded a crocodile farm, allowing over four thousand of the reptiles to escape. Until they were rounded up, people were very careful to keep their pets and children away from the water!

In a 1928 Florida flood caused by a hurricane, several people climbed trees to escape. Some of them died—deadly water moccasin snakes had gotten there first.

WEIRD TALES OF SURVIVAL

In the nineteen thirties, there was a twelve-year-old Virginia boy who always tagged along after his father, sticking to him like a shadow. Nobody ever saw the dad without his son. One rainy night, the father went to get some tools from the workshop near the river behind the house. For some reason, the boy did not follow as he always did. The boy's father didn't come right back, but his mother could see the lights on in the workshop. When the lights went out and he still didn't appear at the back door, she checked. Rapidly rising water had washed the workshop, and her husband, away. His body was found three miles downstream. The question that nobody, including the boy, could ever answer was: What kept him from going out to the tool shed with his dad that night?

A Federal Emergency Management Agency employee tells this story: A West Virginia family wasn't surprised when the creek behind their house began to rise; it happened often. Only the wild barking of their dogs brought them outside to see a raging flash flood. One dog had managed to climb on top of its dog house. The other was desperately swimming at the end of its chain.

The father tied himself to a car, to keep from getting swept away, and waded out to help. He carried the dog from its dog-house roof, but could not reach the dog that was fighting to stay above the raging water. Rather than watch the beloved animal die slowly, the man got his gun and sadly aimed at his faithful dog. On the second shot, it sank beneath the water.

Days passed and the waters receded. A neighbor told them he had seen their dog nearby. Sure it had to be a mistake, the father went to look. To his amazement, he found the dog alive and well, with the chain neatly severed just a few inches from its collar. The man was overjoyed to learn he had missed!

In June, 1972, unusually heavy rains caused a dam to break above Rapid City, South Dakota. As soon as they heard the evacuation order, Shirley and Leo Hessman started to leave. Then Shirley turned back to put their daughter Julie's wedding dress on a high shelf. In those few minutes, the water rose so high they couldn't get out. They spent the night in the attic. Later, they found their Jeep, cut in two by flood debris. Saving the wedding dress probably saved their lives!

LIKELY AND UNLIKELY HEROES

In the Rapid City flood, a patrolman saw a wall of water hit a senior citizens' home. There was no one else around to help, so he worked alone to carry 41 elderly residents to safety through the turbulent water.

In the Johnstown, Pennsylvania, flood, six-year-old Gertrude Quinn was swept away on a mattress. In the roaring water, she was washed close to a floating roof with about 20 people clinging to it. She called out for help. It meant putting himself in deadly peril, but Maxwell McAchren jumped into the water—even though his companions tried to hold him back. Somehow, he made it through the tangle of currents and climbed onto the mattress. He tried to comfort the terrified Gertrude, but could do nothing more to help himself or the little girl.

The floodwater carried them past a nearly submerged building on the bank where men were leaning out an upper story window with long poles, pulling people out of the flood water. Maxwell could only watch—the men were 15 to 20 feet away, too far away to reach the bobbing, turning mattress. Then, one of the men shouted at him to throw the girl to safety.

Maxwell McAchren performed the incredible feat of tossing Gertrude from an unsteady, lurching mattress, straight through an open window into the waiting arms of a rescuer. The current carried him past. This brave and kind man was pulled out of the water further downstream.

Weela the pit bull was only four weeks old when she was dumped in an alley to die. It was a lucky day for her—and a lot of other people and animals—when a kind person found her and took her home. In January 1993, a dam broke, flooding the Tijuana River. Weela's owners went to a friend's ranch to help rescue their twelve dogs.

This sounds much easier than it was. It was pouring rain, making the treacherous currents of water in the flooded area even worse. But Weela led the way and seemed to have had an uncanny ability to sense—and avoid—quicksand, dangerous drop-offs, and mud bogs. If someone needed help she circled back.

Later, seventeen dogs and puppies and a cat were discovered stranded on an island in the flooded river. During the next month, Weela repeatedly swam the river, each time pulling 30 to 50 pounds of dog food in a backpack. Because of her, the marooned animals did not starve before they could be rescued.

And that's not all the amazing Weela did! On one of the rescue swims to the stranded animals, she noticed thirty people trying to cross the treacherous river. She barked, tearing back and forth in front of them to keep them from crossing. Then she led them to a shallower place in the river, where they could cross safely. Weela also led rescuers to thirteen horses that had climbed a huge pile of stable cleanings to stay above the swirling flood. Weela was named Ken-L Ration's Dog Hero of the Year in 1993!

TALL TALES AND DANGEROUS MYTHS

Probably the most dangerous myth about any disaster is the one you hear most often about floods: It could never happen here.

Some areas flood more often than others. People who live next to rivers are usually aware of the danger in rainy years. But always remember sudden heavy rains can turn a desert gully into a deadly torrent of water unbelievably quickly. Even if it is not raining very hard where you are, if it is pouring upstream, water could come roaring down the natural drainage system at any time.

If you are ever in a dry, desert-seeming area and it starts to rain, stay out of gullies and washes. Ask yourself how that gully was formed to start with! Then you will do the sensible thing and run for higher ground.

HOW BAD WAS IT?

The size of a flood is described by how much of

the *floodplain* it covered. That means how much of the land along a river (or lake or stream) is under water. It doesn't take much of a flood to spill over onto the land right next to the river. But the farther out you go on the floodplain, the higher the land gets, and the less chance there is of that land being submerged.

Far enough out, there is land that will probably be flooded only every hundred years. That area is called the 100-year floodplain. When it gets covered with water, the flood is called a 100 Year Flood. That means there is a one in a hundred chance of a flood that size happening each and every year. Since no one can accurately predict weather, or floods, this system is the best way to describe how likely floods of certain sizes will be.

Floods are classified like this:

50-year flood: Likely to happen every fifty years

100-year flood: Likely to happen every hundred years

500-year flood: Likely to happen every five hundred years

How likely? Remember that just because

something has a *chance* of happening every fifty or hundred years, that doesn't mean it *will*. It could happen two years in a row, or not at all.

Here's how it works:

Cut up 100 identically sized pieces of paper—ninety-nine white and one red. Put them in a container and shake them up. Then, without looking, pick one. There is a one in a hundred chance that it will be red. No matter which color it is, put it back and shake the container again. Then, without looking, draw again. There is still a one in 100 chance that it will be red. The *probability* of getting a red one is one in a hundred, or one percent, every time you pick a piece of paper. But you might not get a red one if you draw a hundred times—or you might get two or more—even two or more *in a row*.

WHY, HOW, AND WHERE CAN IT HAPPEN?

Floods can be caused by a number of things: Heavy rains or snow melting too fast; ocean waves coming onshore; or dams or levees breaking. Sometimes floods happen very quickly with almost no warning. These are called flash floods.

When it rains, the ground absorbs the water. But just like a sponge, it can absorb only so much.

Then the water starts running off into streams and rivers. The water level in the rivers starts rising, and if the rain doesn't stop, the river will eventually overflow its banks, flooding the land around it.

THE FLOOD HALL OF FAME

In the last 30 years, an average of 138 people a year have died in floods. Using the number of deaths as a way to rate how bad a flood was, here's the Ten Worst Floods in recent U.S. history:

1. 1889 Johnstown, PA—Burst dam, flood: 2,200–3,000 dead
2. 1913 Indiana and Ohio River Basin—Flood: 467 dead
3. 1927 Mississippi River—Flood: 1,000 dead
4. 1972 Rapid City, SD—Burst dam, flood: 238 dead
5. 1921 Texas—Flood: 215 dead
6. 1903 Heppner, OR—Flash flood: 200 dead
7. 1955 Northeast area—Hurricane, flood: 187 dead
8. 1913 Texas—Flood: 177 dead
9. 1976 Big Thompson—Flood: 145 dead
10. 1977 Johnstown, PA—Burst dam, flood: 85 dead

Property damage in the United States from flooding totals more than $1 billion a year. The 1993 Mississippi flood was classified as a 500-year flood. Because of modern warning systems and transportation, no more than 48 people died.

But warnings and quick evacuation couldn't prevent property damage:

$15–20 billion in property and crop loss

56 small river towns were submerged

85,000 people were evacuated

8,000 homes were destroyed

People's belongings were damaged in 20,000 more homes

404 counties were declared disaster areas

2,000 loaded barges were stranded

700+ graves were opened by floodwater in the Hardin, Missouri, cemetery. Some caskets were washed fourteen miles downstream.

When flood is likely, authorities issue announcements. Here's what you can do if a *Flood Watch* is issued.

- Move valued possessions upstairs, or into an attic.
- Gas up the car, in case you have to evacuate suddenly.
- Fill your bathtub—or plastic or glass bottles—with clean drinking water. Floods often contaminate water supplies.

If the *Flood Watch* announced in your area is a *Flash Flood Watch,* be very alert for early signs of flooding. If you see water running down a gully or pooling in low areas, be ready to evacuate on a moment's notice. You may have only seconds to escape. Act quickly!

An announcement of a *Flood Warning* means a flood is already beginning. Listen to local radio and TV stations for information and advice. If told to evacuate, do so quickly. A *Flash Flood Warning* means to evacuate low ground immediately. Be ready; listen to local newscasts on radio or TV. People killed in floods are sometimes those who go back for precious possessions, or for a pet. Help your family be calm and organized, and get out quickly!

The number one rule for being safe in a flood is simple: Head for high ground, away from rivers, streams, creeks, and storm drains.

Also:

• Don't drive around barricades. They're there for your safety.

• Don't drive across flooded low-water crossings, or anywhere the road dips across a normally dry creek bed. If there are even a few inches of swift water, you might lose control of the car. Water only two feet deep can wash your car away!

• If your car stalls in rapidly rising waters, abandon it immediately! Run to higher ground.

• If you are on foot, never try to cross moving water that is higher than your knees. Remember, the depth at the edge is nearly always less than in the middle of any creek or stream.

• Fast-moving flood water is more forceful than you can imagine, even if it is shallow. The most dangerous thing you can do is to try to walk, swim, or drive through swift water.

• Some freeway underpasses and drainage ditches can carry a flash flood if rainfall is hard enough. Never go beneath an underpass or

into a low-lying area of any kind where water
is starting to collect

TERROR TECHS, WEATHER WIZARDS, AND DISASTER DOCTORS

Floods are studied by meteorologists and hydrologists who analyze water flow. If a career in meteorology or hydrology interests you, talk to a school counselor about getting more information.

Scientists aren't the only flood professionals. Rescuing people from flood waters takes special training and skills far beyond just being a good swimmer. Rescuers understand the awesome power of moving water and the danger of floating debris. An average of three professional rescuers drown each year.

Many firefighters, park rangers, EMS personnel, and other rescue professions are now being trained as "swiftwater rescue technicians." These people become expert in such topics as river physics and hydrology, safety and rescue equipment, shore-based, boat-based, and in-water rescue techniques, helicopter rescue, handling hazards and obstacles, using rescue equipment, setting up rope rescue systems, using teams and rescue dogs, scuba and surface diving.

Rescuing people is a tough and interesting line of work!

During the 1993 flood of the Mississippi, weathermen jokingly called Iowa the sixth Great Lake, because in aerial photos it was hard to tell where Iowa ended and Lake Superior and Lake Michigan began!

The 1889 Johnstown, Pennsylvania, flood was the worst flood in the history of the United States, killing over 2,200 people. But it was not the last deadly flood in Johnstown. In 1977, six dams burst and flooded the town. There is an eerie coincidence about the numbers: In the first Johnstown flood, 777 bodies were buried without being identified. The date of the second flood was 7/77—and it killed 77 people.

When the Guadalupe River flooded and put the ranching town of Victoria, Texas, underwater in 1998, one man went fishing! He sent his family to safety, then stayed behind to move valuables as high as possible. But the flood came too quickly.

He was forced to the roof, grabbing a soda, some shrimp, and two new fishing poles on the way.

From his perch he saw sheep, cows, hogs, even a couple of deer, caught in the floodwater. He watched all sorts of household goods float past. When some of the objects began to look familiar, he started casting his fishing line, trying to hook a good barbecue grill and other prized possessions. How strange he must have felt, stranded on his rooftop, fishing for his belongings!

People in Minnesota are good at making bad times better, too. During a 1991 flood, a farmer took his son waterskiing across a flooded field.

After the Great Flood of the Mississippi River in 1993, in some towns people cleaned up and rebuilt. In other places, the people just moved away. The 900 residents of Valmeyer, Illinois, made an amazing decision. They voted to pick up and move the whole town to higher ground. On a high, safe bluff above the ruins of the old town, they rebuilt Valmeyer from scratch. They constructed hundreds of brand-new houses, a downtown district, churches, a school, a fire station, and a post office.

chapter four

THUNDERSTORMS

imagine this . . .

It is the end of a hot summer day. You are standing in your favorite place—the high school's baseball field. You are pleasantly tired from playing softball with friends. They are getting their bikes, standing around and talking before they leave. You are holding off because you really don't want to go home. Today is the day your mother wants you to clean out the garage.

To the north, a third of the sky has filled with the billowing towers of thunderclouds. They are moving your way, and fast. The little silver flashes tell you it is a lightning storm, and you know that in a few minutes, the storm will be overhead and rain will start to fall. Reluctantly, you get your bike out of the bike stand and walk it slowly across the field. There is a line of cottonwood trees between the field and the street on the far side. As the big drops of rain spatter down, you start to walk faster, heading for the trees.

Lightning splits the sky and thunder crashes almost simultaneously. Instinctively, you duck, knowing the bolt hit somewhere close. As you straighten, you see smoke rising from one of the cottonwoods.

Without thinking, you turn and get on your bike, standing up to pedal back across the open field. As you ride, your breath coming quick and sharp, your heart thudding, you feel a creepy, tickling chill on your neck— as though every hair on your head is standing on end. And you know that there is no time to run and no place to hide.

Acting instantly, you do what your parents have taught you to do. You jump from your bike, whirling to fling the metal frame away from yourself. You tear off your metal framed sunglasses and throw them as far as you can. Then you empty your pockets of coins and heave them away, too. You drop into a catcher's stance, allowing only the balls of your feet to touch the ground. You cover your ears with your hands and wait, heart hammering at your ribs. The tingling feeling gets stronger and stranger. . . .

The U.S. has 100,000 thunderstorms per year, but the odds of an individual being struck by lightning in the United States each year are about 3 million to one. Still, lightning is a killer. Every year in the United States, lightning kills about a hundred people, injures several hundred more, and causes $6 billion of damage.

Lightning is the number 2 weather killer, second only to flood. It kills more people than volcanoes, hurricanes, tornadoes, or earthquakes. People who survive it can have severe, lifelong medical problems.

How do you know if you are about to be struck by lightning? People say they feel like their hair is "standing-on-end" shortly before lightning strikes near them, and sometimes their hair really does stick straight up. Sometimes plastic raincoats start rising up away from the wearer's body.

As a storm approaches, you can determine how far away the lightning is. Sound travels more slowly than light, so you see the lightning before you hear the thunder. When you see the flash, start counting the seconds until you hear the thunder. Sound travels about a mile every five seconds, so divide the number of seconds you counted by five. Five seconds is one mile, ten seconds is two miles, and so forth. Just remember that lightning sometimes strikes "out of the blue" and a long way from the visible storm.

Lightning is smaller than you think, and bigger. Sometimes it's only about an inch in diameter. But lightning more than 100 miles long has been observed.

An average lightning flash has the energy of a one-kiloton explosion. Its voltage is one billion volts. Lightning current averages 30,000 amps, but it ranges from 10,000 to 200,000 amps. That's 100 to 1,000 times as strong as a steel welder.

The temperature of a lightning bolt is about 50,000 degrees Fahrenheit—five times hotter than the surface of the sun. It moves so fast that strike survivors' burns aren't usually very bad. The real damage that lightning does to the human body is caused by the powerful electric current. It makes the heart and lungs stop working. Always start CPR immediately on any lightning victim who looks dead.

Lightning is as bright as about 100 million lightbulbs.

The U.S. has twenty million cloud-to-ground lightning flashes each year. Up to seventy million lightning flashes aloft are also counted.

Lightning is constant. About forty-five thousand thunderstorms happen every day throughout the world. Lightning strikes somewhere on the earth about a hundred times a second. That adds up to eight or nine million strikes a day and about three billion strikes a year worldwide.

In July, 1988, lightning struck near a house in upstate New York. The tires on cars parked in the driveway suddenly went flat, the hubcaps were blown off, and the homeowner's contact lenses popped out.

When you hear thunder, you're hearing the shock wave caused by 70 degree air around the lightning heating to 50,000 degrees in less than a second.

In England a few years ago, a lightning bolt came down a chimney and shot out of the fireplace, passing the family seated in the kitchen, striking the pantry, where it melted the cooking pots together and roasted an uncooked ham.

Lightning over cities is 10 to 20 percent more frequent than over surrounding areas, probably because the air over cities is warmer.

The energy in an average lightning flash could light a 100-watt lightbulb for over three months.

Lightning strikes more people during July than any other month. There are more thunderstorms during July, and many people are at the beach, playing outdoor sports, and engaging in other out-door activities.

In an unusually heavy storm, one lightning bolt killed six elephants as they huddled together in the southern section of the Kruger National Park in South Africa.

Does lightning seek out certain people or families? There's no scientific basis for it, but consider the following:
According to the *Guinness Book of World Records*,

the person who survived the most lightning strikes was former Park Ranger Roy "Dooms" Sullivan. Between 1942 and 1977, he was struck seven times. The first time it went through his leg and knocked his big toenail off. The second time his eyebrows were burnt away and he was knocked out. A year later, lightning burned his shoulder. In 1972, a bolt set his hair on fire. A 1973 strike went through his hat, set his hair on fire, flung him out of his truck, and knocked off his shoe. In 1976, bolt number six injured his ankle, and the last one, in 1977, burned his chest and stomach!

It's All Relative: Between 1921 and 1995, five members of one Midwest family (including cousins, aunts, grandparents, etc.) have been struck by lightning at different times, two of them fatally. One woman was hit twice.

In 1997, on St. Patrick's Day, a Maryland woman was sick in bed when lightning struck her house. It exploded the lightbulb in her bedside lamp. She fled to one of her daughter's homes, but lightning had beaten her to it. A strike had ruined the TV and VCR and started a fire in a baseboard outlet. The woman had another daughter living in another town whom she thought safe. She was wrong. The second daughter's chimney was struck that same day, blasting fireplace bricks across the floor.

In June 1998, during a Scottish golf tournament, lightning struck the tip of one of the player's umbrellas. The player, Father Alex Davie, got under a tree for shelter. A few minutes later, lightning hit the tree while he was still under it. He had a sore arm but kept playing.

As a teenager, a boy named Matthew Nordbrock was stunned by a lightning flash while sitting on a lake in a rowboat. He was not injured, but another boy, who was wearing wire-rimmed glasses, was badly hurt.

Some ten years later, Matthew was wearing metal-framed glasses as he was caught in a thunderstorm at the top of Mount Whitney. He and other climbers ran for shelter in a metal-roofed hut. He joked that he'd been struck by lightning before, so he wouldn't be hit again.

Lightning struck the hut, injuring several of the climbers, but Nordbrock was the only one who was killed. The doctors said it was probably partly because of his metal glasses.

A New York farmer was driving his tractor when he was hit by lightning. He might have survived, but the ambulance taking him to the hospital was hit by lightning, then crashed.

The area around Cape Canaveral is lightning-prone. Storms often delay space launches. During the liftoff of Apollo 12, lightning struck the Saturn V rocket twice, scrambling its electrical systems, but the astronauts were able to regain control of their spacecraft and go on to the moon.

In 1987, a lightning bolt triggered the launch controls of three rockets. One of them shot across the ground the length of a football field and into the ocean. It was carrying instruments designed for studying lightning!

If a rocket carrying an electrical charge plows into a cloud with an opposite charge, the two charges attract each other, and a lightning bolt is triggered. That's why NASA won't launch shuttles if there are any thunderstorms within 10 miles or if clouds are directly overhead. Sometimes scientists use rockets to deliberately trigger lightning so they can study it.

The lightning capital of the world is the West Coast of Africa, where they have thunderstorms up to 295 days out of the year. If you want to avoid lightning, try St. Paul Island in the Bering Sea off Alaska. In 1992, they had their first thunderstorm in forty years.

WEIRD TALES OF SURVIVAL

A boy who survived a lightning strike started having trouble in school in subjects that required spelling and memorizing—like history and reading. But his grades improved in science and math —subjects that rely on thinking in images and concepts. This was the exact reverse of his school performance before the strike!

A couple of English fishermen said that when lightning was about to strike close to them, their hair and their fishing lines rose into the air. They said the tip of a fishing rod buzzed like a swarm of bees.

A weatherman once saw two calmly grazing horses suddenly bolt to the far end of the field for no apparent reason. A few seconds later, a lightning bolt hit the place where they had been standing.

"It was a very intense heat on top of my head," said Scott Shirley, who was grazed by lightning. "It was only on the top area. There was nothing on the sides or the back, and it did feel like my head was on fire."

Harold Deal of Greenville, South Carolina, was struck by lightning in 1969. The lightning ripped the boots off his feet and left two holes in the ground where he was standing. "I had a dollar fifty-something cents in my pocket; it melted," he said. Today, Deal can lie in snow without feeling cold. He has no sense of temperature, taste, or smell, but he is glad to have survived the ordeal!

A climber on Mount Whitney had a round, 4-inch burn on his shoulder where lightning entered his body and burns in at least a dozen places where it exited. There were holes in every piece of clothing he had on except his shoes.

A 1971 traffic accident left Edwin Robinson brain injured—blind and almost deaf. Nine years later, he went out in the rain to bring in his pet chicken. He was carrying an aluminum cane and walked under a tall tree. A bolt of lightning zapped him unconscious for twenty minutes. The amazing truth is that when he came to, he could hear perfectly, and he could see (although he still couldn't move his eyes). Even his bald head soon started growing hair!

Who would stand in a flat, wide open grassy space and wave a metal rod at the sky during a thunderstorm? Thousands of golfers do it every year. Not surprisingly, almost a third of lightning victims are golfers. In 1975, a single lightning bolt knocked Lee Trevino unconscious, jolted Bobby Nichols's club out of his hands, and sent Arnold Palmer's club flying 40 yards down the fairway.

The group of climbers on Mt. Whitney's summit who were struck by lightning sent one of the weirdest distress calls ever made. One climber, less hurt than some of his companions, managed to start down the mountain. As he descended, he found a group of Girl Scouts, who used their radio to call for help. An airliner overhead picked up the signal and relayed it to air traffic controllers in Los Angeles, who contacted the county sheriff, who sent a helicopter to evacuate the climbers.

Ribbon Lightning

Lightning strikes are usually made up of many strokes, all following the same upward channel of ionized air. Extreme winds can sometimes blow the channel of ionized air sideways. This can cause ribbon lightning. It looks like several overlapping strokes, side by side. If you see a photo of lightning that looks like someone jiggled the camera during the shot, but trees, buildings, etc. aren't blurred, you're looking at ribbon lightning.

Bead Lightning

Very rarely, after a big, powerful lightning flash, the lightning seems to break up into a glowing string of balls that look like an eerie bead necklace or a string of sausage links. The beads last much longer than normal lightning. Not much is known about what causes bead lightning. Some parts of the flash must fade faster than others, but nobody knows why.

Bolt from the Blue

"A bolt from the blue" is an old expression that means something comes from nowhere. The saying is based on fact. Just because it isn't raining doesn't mean lightning can't strike. In Arizona, a bolt of lightning killed a man who was playing golf under a clear, sunny sky. The bolt had come from a thunderstorm fifteen miles away.

Ball Lightning

People say that this strange form of lightning follows a normal strike and that it looks like a glowing, floating ball anywhere from two inches in diameter to about the size of a basketball. People claim to have seen ball lightning that was red, white, orange, and yellow—and even blue.

It gets stranger yet. Some people have heard hissing or buzzing sounds as the balls float along a few feet off the ground, meandering, sometimes sinking slowly to the earth. There are claims that the balls have bounced off solid objects. Some people have described them as spinning or rotating.

People say the balls last for a few seconds up to a minute or more, then disappear suddenly, sometimes quietly, sometimes with a popping sound or loud bang. The balls usually don't cause much damage, and some observers have said they seem "playful" or "curious." People don't often feel any heat from the balls, but there has been evidence of melted wires or fires started.

One person watched a glowing ball drop into a pond and described a hissing sound like a hot iron entering the water would make. Another witness saw a ball float into the side of a house, burn the window frame, then land in a tub of water, which started to boil.

Ball lightning has been seen coming down chimneys or floating right through closed glass windows. Usually the window glass isn't damaged, but sometimes the ball melts a neat circular hole as it passes through.

Weirdest of all, there are several reports of airline passengers and crew seeing ball lightning enter an airplane, float around—even roll down the aisle between the seats! Scientists can't explain ball lightning, which may be why some of them don't think it exists.

Ball from the Blue

Two rare kinds of lightning seemed to have combined on April 17, 1999. It was Graham Cooper's first gliding lesson and, in fact, his first day in a glider. The sky was a beautiful blue and about three miles away was an interesting-looking cloud.

Without warning, lightning shot out of the cloud and struck the glider. The right wing exploded. Luckily for Mr. Cooper, the glider club required parachutes.

As the glider spiraled toward the ground and the left wing came off, the instructor, Pete Goldstraw, shouted instructions to Cooper. Once his student was safely away, he bailed out himself. Both men suffered only minor injuries and some hearing loss. This "bolt from the blue" was rare enough, but ground observers insisted the lightning was also in the form of a ball!

TALL TALES AND DANGEROUS MYTHS

Have you heard that lightning never strikes twice in the same place? In fact, it often strikes the same place repeatedly. Because it is so tall, the Empire State Building gets hit many times a year.

In the summer of 1937, a lightning bolt killed three people on a New York beach. Almost exactly a year later, three more people were killed by lightning on the same beach.

A Colorado house was damaged by lightning. Six weeks later, just as repairs were almost finished, the house was struck again, causing another $30,000 worth of damage.

WEIRD EFFECTS OF LIGHTNING

• Sleeping people dream more often during thunderstorms.

• Car engines have been known to stall right before lightning hits nearby. After the strike, the engines can be started easily.

• For centuries, it's been said that sailors rarely hear thunder. Now, night-sky satellite photos show why. More than 85% of lightning is over land. It makes sense. For lightning to form, air must be rising rapidly through the clouds. That can't happen unless the air below the clouds is much warmer than the air above them. Air over water is usually cooler.

• Alaskan lightning usually strikes over forests—not tundra and scrubland. Air temperatures above the forests are higher than above the other types of vegetation.

• Give me back that remote! Lightning often turns on CD players and televisions, especially the kind that can be turned on with an infrared or radio frequency remote control unit.

In 1670, lightning hit a church in Wiltshire, England, cracking the steeple. Three months after it was repaired, lightning hit it again, killing two workers, destroying the steeple, and damaging the church. Almost a hundred years later, the church's vicarage was struck by a bolt of "ball lightning." A vicar was badly hurt.

In 1979, a Tennessee home was destroyed by lightning. It was the third time the house had been hit since being built in 1970.

Hundreds of years ago, there were theories about warding off lightning that included the ringing of church bells. Some thought ringing the bell chased away evil spirits. Others thought the noise disrupted the lightning strokes. Both theories made bell ringing a very dangerous occupation.

During one thirty-three-year period in the 1700s, lightning struck 386 French church towers and killed 103 French bell ringers. On Good Friday, 1718, all twenty-four bell-ringing churches in lower Brittany were struck. The six that remained silent were not hit. Seventy years later, the French government outlawed the custom. The lightning rod had finally been invented.

At Christmas in some parts of Germany, people used to burn a large oak log just until it was charred, then pulled it off the fire. Once it was cool, they would put it under the bed, and save it for stormy weather. Then they'd put it back on the fire, believing that burning a Yule log protected the house from lightning.

The ancient Greeks and Romans believed that lightning could not strike the bay laurel tree, so they often wore its leaves to ward off strikes.

Putting an acorn on the window sill was supposed to keep lightning out of the house.

Mirrors were said to attract lightning so people covered them during storms.

Mistletoe and holly, now traditional Christmas greenery, were once thought to protect a house from lightning.

Some people used to think that lightning wouldn't strike people who were asleep or that it would pass through them harmlessly.

Feather beds were supposed to provide protection from lightning.

Some people carried a piece of wood from a tree struck by lightning because they believed "lightning won't strike the same tree twice." Toothpicks from lightning trees were thought to cure toothache.

SAFETY MYTHS: TRUE OR FALSE?

MYTH: People who have been struck by lightning are electrically charged afterward.

False: It is safe—and necessary—to check immediately to see if they are breathing and if their hearts are beating, and start CPR if necessary.

MYTH: Rubber-soled shoes will protect you from lightning.

False: Air is almost as good an insulator as rubber. Lightning has traveled miles through the atmosphere. It isn't going to be stopped by a half inch of rubber.

THE TRUTH (about Benjamin Franklin's kite): Most people know about Ben Franklin flying a kite in a thunderstorm to prove that lightning was electrical. That much is true. But it is NOT true that lightning struck his kite. If it had, it probably would have killed him instantly.

Franklin's experiment proved some storm clouds carry strong electrical charges. His kite and string collected a tiny bit of that charge from the cloud, causing the hairs on the twine to stick outward.

Franklin also charged up a metal key by touching it to the twine and showed that he could get tiny sparks from the key. This indicated that lightning was probably just a big electric spark. NEVER TRY FRANKLIN'S EXPERIMENT YOURSELF! It is very dangerous. Franklin was lucky he wasn't killed!

WHY, HOW, AND WHERE CAN IT HAPPEN?

The formation of lightning is similar to the sparks that leap between your fingers and a metal doorknob if you have scuffed your shoes across the carpet.

When atoms in a storm cloud lose or gain electrons, they become electrically charged. Those that lose an electron have a positive charge; those that gain an electron have a negative charge. They are all called ions.

Usually, negative ions gather at the bottom of the cloud and positive ions at the top. An attraction builds between the negative underside of a cloud and any positive ions that happen to be around. When the attraction is strong enough, a lightning bolt, which is really a huge spark, jumps across the gap.

If the positive ions are at the top of a cloud, the spark jumps between clouds. If they are on the surface of the earth, the spark hits the earth.

Here is one of the Freakiest Facts of all: Lightning bolts usually go up from the earth, not down from the cloud. As a lightning flash is starting to form, a small, almost invisible streamer of negative ions called a "stepped leader" moves from the cloud toward the Earth, trying to find the best way to get to the positive ions down there. It often forms branches on its way down, as it tries one path, then another.

On the ground, positive ions gather at the strike point and start streaming upward. The ions move toward each other at 200,000 miles an hour. When the two streams connect, the electrical circuit is complete, and the charge from the ground surges upward along the same path at close to the speed of light. It moves so fast that the air around it heats up and glows, and we see the bright flash of lightning. The super-heated air explodes outward, producing a shock wave that we hear as thunder.

Multiple strokes usually follow the same path, over and over, for up to a quarter of a second or more. That's why lightning seems to flicker.

Lightning can be forked. As the stepped leader makes its way toward the earth, it moves in fits and starts, looking for the best way to get through the air, which actually makes a pretty good insulator. It moves about 30 yards, stops, and moves again. When it stops, it might branch into two different paths before starting downward again. The branches meet the upward-bound streamer from the earth, a bright flash is generated for each branch. It all happens so fast that what you see is one spectacular flash of forked lightning.

Where you are can make a difference in the odds that you will ever be struck by lightning. The central coast of California is the least likely place in the United States. Clearwater, Florida, is the lightning capital of the U.S., with the highest rate of lightning strikes per capita.

THE LIGHTNING HALL OF FAME

May 7, 1937: The *Hindenberg* airship was destroyed by an electrostatic discharge that ignited the flammable airtight coatings, and 97 people died.

July 10, 1926: Lightning exploded a navy ammunition depot in Mount Hope, New Jersey, killing 19 people and wounding 38.

June, 1998: Despite the fact that lightning rods had been installed, lightning struck an outdoor rock concert with 35,000 people in Baltimore, Maryland, injuring 13 people.

July, 1998: Five firefighters were injured when lightning struck their fire truck in Las Vegas, Nevada.

In 1988 nine girls in Tustin, California, were hurt when lightning struck the tree under which their softball team had taken shelter from the rain.

October, 1998: Lightning killed all 11 members of one soccer team in Congo, Africa. The opposing team was unharmed.

LIFESAVING FACTS

Go inside and stay inside.

This is the number one safety rule. Lightning victims are usually outdoors. Many are playing golf or field sports like baseball or soccer, or are near a lake, swimming pool, or other water. It's possible to be struck indoors, but far less likely.

Once you are inside:

Stay away from windows.

It's easier for lightning to go through glass than through walls. Don't touch metal windows or door frames.

Don't use handheld electrical appliances.

Wait until the storm is over to dry your hair or talk on the phone. Lightning can travel through electrical wires and phone wires. Don't use a head-set or play video games.

Stay away from water.

Don't wash your hands. Lightning can travel through water pipes.

If you can't get indoors:

Don't stand under a tree.

Running under a tree to get out of the rain is one of the most dangerous things you can do in a storm. Even if you aren't touching the tree when lightning strikes it, the lightning can reach you through the ground or come straight down from the branches. If the tree explodes you can be injured by flying pieces of wood. Tall, single trees are most dangerous. If you are in thick woods, find a stand of small trees if you can.

Get away from water.

If you are swimming, get out of the water the minute you hear thunder or see dark clouds or lightning in the distance. If you are in a boat, head for shore.

Avoid wide, flat open spaces like ball parks and golf courses.

Avoid metal.

Don't stand near metal fences, power lines, farm equipment, etc. These things attract lightning. Get rid of any metal you are carrying and don't wait until your hair is standing on end and you hear crackling noises! When you hear thunder, make a mental list. Does your backpack have a metal frame? Do you have keys and coins in your pocket? Do you have a metal donut on your baseball bat?

Are you wearing shoes with metal spikes or taps? Glasses? Earrings? A watch? If lightning comes close, don't just drop your metal possessions— throw them as far as you can. Or set them down and run away from them if you have time.

Get down.

Find the lowest ground you can that isn't near water. Then, if you can, get into a catcher's stance. Balance in a crouch with just the balls of your feet touching the ground. The idea is to minimize your contact with the ground. Put your hands over your ears to protect your eardrums from the thunder.

Pay attention to weird feelings.

Sometimes people get a "hair-standing-on-end" feeling right before lightning strikes. If you ever get that feeling while you are outside during a thunderstorm, you are in danger. The tingle means lightning is considering you as a possible route to the ground. React immediately! It might save your life.

If you are in a car:
Tell the driver to pull over and park, turn on

the blinkers, and turn off the engine. STAY IN THE CAR if it has a metal body.

Don't touch anything metal, like door handles, gearshifts, steering wheel, and radio knobs. Put your hands in your lap and wait for the storm to end. You are fairly well protected from lightning in a car or school bus, as long as you don't touch any metal parts. Sometimes, police officers' hands and mouths have gotten badly burned because they were using their radio microphones when lightning hit their cars.

Many people think the rubber tires protect them in a car. They're wrong. They are safer in a car because the electric current runs over the outside of the car body instead of through it to the interior. This is sometimes called the "skin effect" and it is common when lightning strikes airplanes. You are not protected in a convertible, in a fiberglass or plastic car, or on a motorcycle, riding lawn mower, or golf cart. Leave these vehicles and seek cover nearby.

If you are in an airplane:

Surprisingly, you are quite safe from lightning when you are in an airplane, even though you might be right up there where the lightning is forming. The many crashes associated with thunderstorms are caused by wind shear and wild turbulence, not lightning.

In 1963 lightning struck a Pan American airplane over Elkton, Maryland, and ignited fumes from the fuel tank. After that crash, fuel tanks have been redesigned to keep out electrical charges. Lightning hasn't caused a major crash since.

The average airliner gets hit by lightning twice a year. Passengers and crew are safe because all the electrical current travels along the outside metal skin of the airplane. It usually runs from nose to tail or from wing tip to wing tip, discharging harmlessly in the air.

TERROR TECHS, WEATHER WIZARDS, AND DISASTER DOCTORS

Most lightning research focuses on what happens above ground and is done by meteorologists who have specialized in lightning studies. But there are scientists who dig lightning bolts out of the ground.

Lightning doesn't stop when it hits the earth. When it strikes soil, especially hard-packed sandy soil, it sometimes melts the sand, leaving behind long hollow tubes of glass called *fulgurites*. The longest one found so far has three branches that are eight, fourteen, and sixteen inches long. Studying fulgurites will help scientists learn how to protect underground power lines from lightning strikes.

There is also research being done from above the clouds. NASA uses high altitude airplanes to study the electrical and optical characteristics of lightning. Capable of altitudes of 12 miles, the planes can fly over huge thunderstorms and have provided a great deal of information about lightning.

There are hobbyist storm chasers who track down and photograph lightning, fascinated with capturing the amazing phenomenon on film. One well-known lightning photographer, David O. Stilling, began his career twenty years ago as a sunset photographer. Since he lived in Florida, the lightning capital of the United States, storm clouds were always interfering. Driving home after one storm-ruined sunset, he caught a glimpse of a lightning bolt in his rearview mirror. He stopped to see if he could get a picture of lightning, and has been chasing storms to shoot lightning bolts ever since.

People say you have about as much chance of winning a big lottery as you have of getting struck by lightning. A man in Orange County, California was hospitalized for lightning injuries. A visitor asked if he needed anything and he replied, "Well, you might pick me up a lottery ticket."

You should never stand next to the tallest object around in a thunderstorm—but you can double that warning in the desert. There, the tallest object is sometimes a huge Saguaro cactus. Some are fifty feet tall and can absorb up to 500 gallons of water. When lightning hits them, the water instantly vaporizes. The cactus explodes, hurtling spiked shrapnel in every direction.

chapter five

DROUGHT

imagine this . . .

For five years your family's Kansas farm has been boom-
ing. The prices of wheat and corn have risen and every
year has brought a good harvest—and more fields planted
the following spring. Your mother was able to remodel the
kitchen last year, and your father is driving a shiny new
truck. It seems like all their hard work and effort are pay-
ing off. Things could hardly be better.

But then in 1931, the rain just stops. At first, every-
one keeps saying it'll be a few more days or a few more
weeks at most, but the days pass and it does not rain. It
does not rain for five long years.

In the first year, the ground turns to dust, and as the
drought continues, all the fields that had been green with
wheat and corn stand empty and brown, the topsoil
swirling in the whirlwinds that crisscross the fields.

Two years later, women have learned to hang laundry
indoors so the clothes are not red with dust by the time
they are dry. They stuff rags beneath doors and along
window sills to keep out some of the dust. Your mother no

longer leaves the lid off simmering soup, and when she makes bread, she kneads it down inside a drawer—left open just far enough to accommodate her two hands.

Once in a while, there is a clear, windless day: not often enough. Almost every day is a battle with the dust. You hear your mother crying in the kitchen sometimes. Your father looks tired and worried all the time. There is always grit in your eyes and your mouth. There is no escape from the dust. Every night you go to bed feeling hopeless and defeated.

Your father's savings are nearly gone. You would quit school and find work if you could—but no one is hiring any help. Every farm in the state is as dry and barren as your family's. Some people are picking up and moving away, tying everything they still own atop their beat-up farm trucks. The ugly, dust-colored wind seems to blow them down the roads, as forlorn and helpless as tumbleweeds.

One morning, the day dawns clear and bright, and your spirits rise. Your parents decide to go to town, leaving you in charge of your little brother. By noon it is ninety degrees, the hottest day of the whole summer. But an hour later, the temperature is dropping weirdly, falling to 40 degrees in a few hours.

You go on with your chores because you don't know what else to do. You start to clean the cow pen, glancing at the sky every few seconds. Your little brother is quiet, and you know he is wondering what's wrong. You hope he won't ask because you don't have an answer. You notice flocks of birds gathering in the cottonwood trees by the barn. They are chattering nervously, staying close together. Seeing them makes you feel even more uneasy.

At about 2:30, you see something strange—a boiling mass of darkness on the horizon is coming closer with frightening speed. You drop the manure shovel and call for your brother to stay close. Dragging your brother along, you run for the house, but the raging darkness closes over you at the edge of the yard. You are surrounded by choking dust—blinded and deafened by it. Your heart slamming in your chest, you begin to crawl, praying that you are going the right direction. Eyes squeezed shut, you hear your brother screaming your name and choking on the dust. When your hand touches the porch steps, you cry out in relief.

Inside the house, the wind howling outside, the dust is so thick that it is visible, a dirty haze that swirls and eddies, as the winds find their way through the walls. For almost four hours, the winds rage, the 7,000-foot-high roil of dust blackening the sky. The radio won't work; the signal's jammed by the static electricity generated by billions of dust particles rubbing together.

You peek out the back door only once. Grit and sand sting your eyes, blinding you instantly. Your brother helps drag the door closed against the raging winds. You slide to the floor, your back against the wall, and try not to cry because you know it will frighten your little brother even more. You close your aching, grit-filled eyes and pray that your parents are all right.

Finally, at about six that evening, the winds subside. There is a weird, yellowish-orange glow to the west. The howling of the winds is gone, replaced by an eerie stillness. You shove open the door and find the porch deep in flour-fine dust.

In the yard, you see a strange dog, lying dead. Just beyond it is one of the cows, lying still on its side, its neck twisted at an odd angle. You rub your eyes, trying to make sense of the scene, but you can't. The whole world is changed, everything coated in ugly brown, the fences buried, drifts of dust piled against the sides of the sheds and the barn.

When your parents finally make it home, you have begun sweeping the house, but it will be days of hard work before your family can eat or sleep without the dust seeping into food and bedclothes. Your parents look around the yard and you can see tears in your father's eyes. Your mother's face is pale and bleak. The wind and dust have destroyed the farm they have worked so hard to build. When the radio works again you will all learn that your drought has been given a catchy name by a newspaperman. Announcers are calling it the Dust Bowl.

Drought doesn't appear with a crash of thunder, the roar of wind, or an electrical light show. "What a gorgeous weekend," people say. "I was afraid it was going to rain, but look at that sunny sky!" But drought is a disaster, just like its noisier, more dramatic relatives, and sometimes even more deadly.

Hundreds of people die from the awful heat that comes with drought, especially old people and young children. In the terrible 1980 heat wave, more than 1,250 people died.

The real killer that drought brings is famine. Without rain, crops can't grow and livestock die. In the late 1960s and 1970s, a drought in the Sahel region of Africa killed more than 100,000 people and several million cattle. In 1877 and 1878, over 9 million Chinese people died in a drought.

In the early 1970s, Arlington, Texas, got so dry that city officials had to mow the grass growing in the exposed and still damp bottom of Lake Arlington.

The August 1998 drought in central Texas caused the soil under houses to shift, leading to broken foundations and plumbing. Residents were advised to water the bases of their houses with a hose every night.

The Texas summer of August 1998 was so hot and dry that shy wild animals came into neighborhoods in search of water. People found foxes and skunks in their swimming pools, raccoons drinking from their pets' water bowls, and rats frolicking in freshly watered gardens.

Life was miserable during the drought that became known as the Dust Bowl. People sealed up their houses. They used knives to wedge rags and newspaper into cracks around doors and windows. Many tried hanging wet sheets over the window frames. Nothing really helped. The dust sifted into their homes as though it was coming straight through the walls.

The dust filled dishes in closed cupboards, settled on clothes *inside* closets—it even got into food kept inside sealed ice boxes.

In the Dust Bowl, there were ceilings that collapsed under the weight of dust that had filled attics.

In 1935, at a college basketball game in Hayes, Kansas, dust sifted through the skylights. It was so thick that the players couldn't see all the way across the floor from one basket to the other. The game was stopped every few minutes so that the floor could be swept—so that the players could see the court lines!

One man remembers visiting relatives during a sandstorm. Everyone went to bed; the dust darkened the sky so that they couldn't do much else. He pulled the sheet over his head to protect his eyes and nose from the dirt. The next morning, the sheet was so weighted with dust he had a hard time getting up.

Severe dust storms—called "black rollers" or "black blizzards" darkened daytime into midnight. They came in like dry, black tidal waves. Some of them were thousands of feet high. They often struck so suddenly that people had no time to seek shelter.

The worst dust storm was probably May 10, 1934. It came from the west, and it was nine hundred miles wide and fifteen hundred miles long. Places as far east as Washington, D.C., were showered with dirt. An estimated twelve million tons of soil fell on Chicago the next day. The dust darkened daytime skies enough to fool chickens into going to roost.

The roiling dust of black rollers was incredibly dangerous. People trying to find cover were often completely lost within shouting distance of their own front doors. One man was caught out on his tractor. He had lived on his farm 50 years but was unable to figure out where he was until he finally ran into a water tank in the farmyard.

Dust storms sometimes had very eerie effects. Millions of dust particles rubbing against each other generated static electricity. It was enough to jam radio broadcasts. Drivers sometimes couldn't start their cars because all the static electricity in the air shorted out their ignitions. The heat from the static electricity sometimes cooked crops right in the field. Balls of electricity would dance up radio antennas. Sparks sometimes traveled along barbed wire fences. Windmill blades turning in the dust sparked enough to look like sparklers on the Fourth of July.

Dust storms left deep drifts of "imported" dirt that, unlike snowdrifts, wouldn't melt! The dust buried tractors, animals, buildings, and fences. Sometimes only a few inches of the fence posts remained above the dirt drifts. Some farmers dug them up and then replaced them at the new, higher, ground level.

People who survived dust storms sometimes swallowed so much dust that they had to vomit clumps of mud afterwards.

The combination of airborne dust and the wet sheets hung to trap it caused a disease that was named "dust pneumonia." It could be fatal if not treated and was worst among babies who slept in cribs covered with wet sheets.

A Kansas veterinarian did an autopsy on a cow and found that her stomach had so much dirt in it that a tumbleweed was growing inside it.

After dust storms, people were sometimes found unconscious in their own yards. Farmers often strung waist-high clothesline from their houses to their barns. They were afraid of getting lost between the barn and the house in the next dust storm.

The Dust Bowl had one weird effect no one seems able to explain: jackrabbits were everywhere. There seemed to be one of the long-eared creatures in the shade of every fence post. The hungry rabbits plagued farmers, leaving almost nothing green standing above the ground. They even chewed holes in people's curtains. Farmers, struggling to feed their families in the hard times, often brought home rabbits for supper.

By the end of the 1930s, 3.5 million people had fled the drought-stricken Great Plains. They loaded old trucks and cars with everything they owned and headed west, hoping to find jobs. They left behind 10,000 empty, unsalable houses and 9 million acres of abandoned farmland.

WEIRD TALES OF SURVIVAL

During a "black roller" one lucky man knew he was only a few feet from his front porch. Even though he could not see or hear in the raging dust-choked wind, he managed to crawl forward slowly until he found it.

In one dust storm, it took a family two and a half hours to drive seven miles home, even with people hanging out the windows to help direct the driver along a road they could barely see.

For most people, especially in earlier eras, surviving a drought became a grinding experience that slowly exhausted and demoralized the drought victims. In many places in the world, drought means famine. Few families in the Dust Bowl starved to death, though some came close. But even families with enough to eat suffered day in and day out.

Housewives had to battle the dust every day:

When cooking food, lids were lifted for only a few seconds—to keep dust out. Bread was kneaded inside drawers, and laundry hanging to dry was often muddied by dusty winds.

All water was kept sealed in jars—or it would become red mud as dust settled into it.
Bed sheets were hung from the ceiling to trap floating dust.

Tables were set "up-side-down." The plates and glasses were turned over to keep out the dust until the family sat down to eat. Even then, the food usually tasted gritty. Before the end of the meal, there was often enough dust on the plates to "draw" in with a fingertip.

Babies' cribs were usually covered with cloth to keep the dust from smothering infants. Many older children slept with wet cloths over their nose and mouths. Every morning, sheets and pillow cases were shaken out to get rid of the night's sand and dust.

The winds changed direction often. Sweeping their floors, Kansas housewives could always tell which state the dirt came from. Reddish dust meant the soil had been blown in from Oklahoma on a southern wind. The west winds brought the black dirt from the plains of Colorado.

Old bed sheets were often torn into pieces, wet, then fastened over closed windows. One Oklahoma woman recalls having to wash the mud out of the damp sheets several times a day.

HOW BAD WAS IT: SCALES AND MEASURES

A *drought* is a period of time without rain that

lasts long enough to affect crops. But how do you know if you're having one? It depends on where you live. What might be a drought in one place could be a deluge in another. On the tropical island of Bali, a drought is defined as a period of six days without rain!

To tell if you're having a drought, you have to compare the current year's rainfall to what your area normally gets. If you normally get 50 inches of rain, and this year you get only 25 inches, then rainfall was 50% of normal.

Drought is also measured by the Palmer Drought Severity Index (PDSI). This index measures both abnormally dry—and abnormally wet—weather. A positive number means more rain than normal, and a negative one means less than normal.

PALMER DROUGHT SEVERITY INDEX

4.00 or more	Extremely wet
3.00 to 3.99	Very wet
2.00 to 2.99	Moderately wet
1.00 to 1.99	Slightly wet
0.50 to 0.99	Incipient wet spell
0.49 to –0.49	Near normal
–0.50 to –0.99	Incipient dry spell
–1.00 to –1.99	Mild drought

−2.00 to −2.99	Moderate drought
−3.00 to −3.99	Severe drought
−4.00 or less	Extreme drought

WHY, HOW, AND WHERE CAN IT HAPPEN?

Droughts can happen almost anywhere on earth. No one knows exactly what causes some years to bring more rain than others, but it is thought that ocean currents, like the famous El Niño, have some effect.

Anywhere that has too little rain some years is a potential drought area. If the rain-scant years come close together, the land can dry out, crops can fail, and high winds can stir powder-dry soil.

The drought that became known as the Dust Bowl was made worse by forces other than a failure of rainfall. After all, the Great Plains had seen wind and drought many times over thousands of years. Before the coming of the American farmer, though, things had been different. The land had been covered with buffalo grass that held moisture and kept the soil from blowing away.

By the early 1900s, homesteaders and farmers started plowing the buffalo grass under to create new fields to plant. They used a new invention— the farm tractor—to plow larger and larger areas.

Without the strong roots of the buffalo grass and other native plants to hold it, the soil blew away when the first drought came.

Drought is very different from other kinds of weather disasters. Hurricanes last only days or weeks. Flood waters usually subside within hours or days. Tornadoes are usually gone in minutes. But a drought can last for years or decades or even, scientists think, centuries. Other disasters usually affect smaller areas than droughts do, too. The 1988 drought affected 36% of the United States, and the Dust Bowl of the 1930s affected 75% of the United States. Every year, some part of the United States suffers extreme or severe drought. In dollars, the yearly losses caused by drought are $6 billion to $8 billion.

THE DROUGHT HALL OF FAME

The worst U.S. drought ever recorded was probably the Dust Bowl of the 1930s. The worst drought in recent United States history was the 1988–89 drought, which cost $40 billion in agricultural losses. The drought caused between 5,000 and 10,000 deaths, including those related to heat stress.

Recent droughts that have cost over a billion dollars:

June–September 1980: Central and Eastern U.S. About $20 billion damage.

Fall 1995 through Summer 1996: Southern plains, especially Texas and Oklahoma. About $5 billion damage.

Summer 1993: Southeastern U.S. About $1 billion damage. South Carolina lost over 95% of its corn crop, and 1.8 million chickens died from the heat. It was the hottest July on record for many parts of the Southeast. Some places had no measurable rain for over sixty days.

LIFESAVING FACTS

In very hot weather, slow down. Reduce strenuous activity, or eliminate it if you can. Stay in the coolest place you can, outdoors or indoors. Remember: lightweight, light-colored clothing reflects heat and sunlight and helps you stay cool. Drink water and other nonalcoholic fluids even if you don't feel thirsty. If you have epilepsy or heart, kidney, or liver disease, or have a problem with fluid retention, consult a doctor before you drink excessive water. Don't take salt tablets unless your doctor tells you to. Spend more time in air-conditioned places. If your home doesn't have air conditioning, consider going to a mall or to stores that do. Don't get too much sun. Sunburn makes it even harder for your body to cool itself.

If you feel dizzy, clammy and chilly, or weak, immediately find shelter from the sun and drink fluids. Tell your companions you are feeling sick from the heat so they can keep an eye on you. Heatstroke can kill. Heat exhaustion or heat stroke should be treated by a doctor.

TERROR TECHS, WEATHER WIZARDS, AND DISASTER DOCTORS

Scientific measurements of drought go back only about a hundred years, and some scientists don't think that is long enough to use the data to predict future droughts. They think drought cycles are measured by decades and centuries, not years! People who study ancient climate changes are called paleoclimatologists.

They are trying to piece together rainfall patterns for the last two thousand years in places like the drought-prone Great Plains of the United States. They take tiny core samples from ancient trees like the bristlecone pine, some of which are thousands of years old. In rainy years, core samples show wide growth rings. In drought years, the trees grew less, so the rings are narrow.

The paleoclimatologists also dig through soil and rock layers to examine ancient pollen, fossils, archeological remains, and lake and river sediments. For more recent information, they study old letters, farm records, or anything else that might mention droughts in the past.

Putting together this vast puzzle of data, paleoclimatologists have discovered something frightening. Droughts like the Dust Bowl seem to happen about twice a century. Worse, there's evidence of "megadroughts" that come every few hundred years. These droughts last for *decades*.

There was a megadrought in the 1500s and one in the 1200s. Amazingly, there seems to have been a drought that began around the year 750 and lasted for *centuries*. Are we due for another megadrought? That's what paleoclimatologists are trying to figure out.

FRIGHTFULLY FUNNY AND SERIOUSLY STRANGE

One of the strangest things about droughts is that people *aren't* too serious to make jokes. In fact, people have always found that a sense of humor helps them survive terrible disasters, especially in disasters that go on for years. Here's some of the bitter, but still frightfully funny, jokes that came out of the Dust Bowl:

A drop of water hit a farmer in the face and he fainted. They had to throw three buckets of sand on him to bring him around.

Texas housewives went on strike and refused to clean house. They said they'd agreed to make their homes in Texas and didn't see why they had to sweep Kansas wheat fields.

A man picked up a hat he found lying on a dusty road and was shocked to see a head under it. He offered to help dig the man out, but the man said, "Oh, that's all right. I'm driving a truck."

Because so many of them were from Oklahoma, people who migrated to California with what was left of their belongings piled onto their car were called "Okies." There were Californians who made up unkind jokes like this one: "How do you tell a rich Okie? He has TWO mattresses on top of his car."

Every morning, store owners had to sweep the piles of dirt away from their doors to open them. One morning, a Kansas hardware store owner swept all the dirt into a pile and stuck a sign in it reading, "Oklahoma farmland for sale."

Sometimes the wind would blow for days without letting up. People joked that if the wind stopped suddenly, all the chickens would fall over.

People claimed that there was so much dirt in the air that prairie dogs were seen burrowing in it.

Nebraska farmers complained that the wind blew so hard their chickens were laying the same eggs two or three times.

People said it was so dry that:
—the trees were whistling for the dogs. One big elm tree even chased a dog down Main Street in a Texas town.

—a sad Texan prayed, "I wish it would rain—
not so much for me, I've seen it—but for my
7-year-old."

—the cows gave powdered milk.

—a man bet several of his friends that it
never would rain again, and collected from
two of them.

chapter six

HURRICANES

imagine this . . .

It's Sunday, September 18, 1938, and you are listening to the radio in the living room while your mother starts making supper. It's the second week of school on Long Island, New York, and you are trying to adjust to the idea that summer is over by looking at your math textbook.

The radio crackles, then the cloth-covered speaker blares out an advertisement for hair oil. You turn the page of your math book. A few minutes later, the word "Miami" catches your ear and you lay down your math book and turn to hear the rest of a news broadcast. The announcer is warning of a hurricane, closing in on the Florida city where your aunt and uncle live.

You jump up to tell your mother. She wipes her hands on her apron and heads to the telephone to turn the crank and get the operator.

"Tilly says not to worry," your mother tells you a moment or two later, fitting the receiver back into the prongs of the phone cradle. "They're boarding up the

windows and she says they will ride it out like they have the past eight or ten." She shakes her head. "I am glad we moved up here. A thousand miles away is exactly how I like my hurricanes."

You ask her if there has ever been a hurricane on Long Island. She smiles. "A hundred and twenty-odd years ago there was one. Not since." You feel a knot in your stomach loosen and go back to your math text.

Monday evening, you listen to the news again before you start your homework. The storm did not come close to Miami and the danger is over, the announcer says. The storm has turned out to sea. You sigh in relief and go back to memorizing the Gettysburg Address. By Friday you are to have it word-perfect.

Wednesday at school, you hear kids talking about the big waves. Walking home, you cut over to the beach and see for yourself. They are huge! The white crests are beautiful. Even with most of the wealthy summer people gone back to their city homes for the year, the beaches aren't empty. Lots of people are out watching the high surf, the wind whipping the women's scarves.

By the time you get home, the wind is blowing so hard that you have to hang onto the front door to keep it from being slammed into the wall when you open it. Once inside, you hear the whistle of the wind as it scrapes past the eaves.

Your parents are standing together in the living room looking out the window. They turn when you come in, and your father's face looks bleak and tight. He tells you to stay inside. You nod, feeling the knot in your stomach tightening again.

An hour later, the sky has turned black and rain is falling in wind-driven sheets. You can see birds in the lightning flashes, flying frantically, being blown backward! Your father yells at you to come away from the window. As you turn you see what looks like a bank of fog rolling through the houses on the far side of the street. Then you realize it's water. . . .

When these ferocious storms are in the Atlantic and Northeastern Pacific, people call them hurricanes. The same kind of storms are called typhoons in the Northwestern Pacific, willy-willies in the Southwestern Pacific, and baquiros in the Philippines.

The word hurricane comes from the Spanish word *huracán,* which probably came from the languages of indigenous people as *Hunraken,* the Mayan god of storms, or *Hurakan,* a Qiche deity of thunder and lightning—or a number of other similar words from peoples who lived in the theater of the huge storms.

Hurricanes have always plagued sailors. During one 1845 hurricane off the U.S. mid-Atlantic coast, more than 50 ships were known to be within about 450 miles of the storm's center. In 1875–76, "heavy weather" sank 176 steamships. From 1840 to 1893, 7,523 people died in 125 North Atlantic steamship disasters. Many were hurricane-caused.

In 1837 a hurricane wrecked thirty-six ships in an east coast harbor. Over 100 seamen drowned within sight of safety. Between 1790 and 1850 three out of every five sailors off New England drowned. Many were killed in hurricanes at sea.

Snakes are a serious danger in hurricanes. People who climb trees to escape a rising storm surge often find they have company slithering in the branches. A Texas A&M study suggests that most people who drowned in 1957's Hurricane Audrey had fallen, snake-bitten, from the trees they had climbed.

In 1992, a ceramic piggy bank in Florida came through Hurricane Andrew unbroken, though the shed it had been in was destroyed. The same family recovered a wedding picture from a woman sifting debris from mud a mile away!

These three states hold the record for multiple hurricane hits: In 1955, North Carolina was hit with hurricanes CONNIE, DIANE, and IONE. Florida suffered in 1964 from CLEO, DORA, and HILDA. In 1985 ELENA, DANNY, and JUAN smashed Louisiana.

In October of 1988 Hurricane Joan moved

along the north coast of South America, then slammed into Central America. Its 135 mph wind caused the worst national disaster ever in Nicaragua. Then, Joan moved across Central America into the Pacific—a first! The storm was then a tropical cyclone and was renamed MIRIAM—another first.

1992's Hurricane Andrew caused only two boating-related deaths in southeast Florida. Radio warnings and coast guard efforts have made a huge difference. People escaped; their boats didn't. There was over half a billion dollars in damage.

In this century, only 1907 and 1914 were hurricane-free in the Atlantic, Caribbean, and Gulf of Mexico. In 1969 there were twelve hurricanes.

Storm surge is an ocean swell caused by the driving winds of the hurricane and the strange shifts in air pressure they cause. Sometimes the surge is as high as 20 to 30 feet. Storm surge usually rises slowly to its peak, then flows out in 6 to 12 hours. But sometimes it's sudden and floods low islands, docks, and waterfront buildings. Rolling ashore on top of the storm surge are battering, dangerous waves. In the U.S., storm surge causes 90% of hurricane-related fatalities. Storm surge is a killer.

The average hurricane damage per year in mainland U.S. is $4.8 billion!

Geologists think there are layers of sediment at the bottom of a lake in Alabama deposited by storm surges from hurricanes over the Gulf of Mexico—as long as 3,000 years ago!

The first human record of Atlantic hurricanes might be a Mayan hieroglyph. These Indians built their major settlements far from the hurricane-battered coastlines. They were smart! Most hurricane damage is to our waterfront cities.

In 1609, ships carrying settlers from England to Virginia sailed into a hurricane. Some ships were damaged; some were stranded in Bermuda, and the people settled there. Their stories of survival may have helped inspire Shakespeare's *The Tempest*.

Sometimes, hurricanes change history. The French attempt to control the Atlantic coast faltered when a 1565 hurricane scattered their fleet.

In 1640, a hurricane damaged the Dutch fleet poised to attack Havana. In 1666, Lord Willoughby, British Governor of Barbados, lost most of his seventeen ships and nearly 2,000 troops in a hurricane.

In November 1970, a tropical cyclone with waves five stories high hit East Pakistan, killing more than 500,000 people. Angry survivors revolted, blaming the government for not warning them and for too-slow rescue and help efforts. They founded their own country: Bangladesh. In May 1991, another hurricane struck. Millions still lived in Bangladesh's low-lying coastal plain and mud flats. There were no tall buildings or high ground to escape to, and hundreds of thousands of people were killed.

President McKinley once commented on the Spanish American War, saying he feared a hurricane more than the Spanish Navy. He helped motivate a reworking of the U.S. hurricane warning service, a forerunner of today's National Hurricane Center.

Strange, but true: In the middle of a hurricane

is a circle of clear weather. There's little or no rain; sometimes blue sky or stars are visible. This clear-weather "eye" can be 120 miles across, but is usually 20 to 40 miles across. It's surrounded by a cloud layer, called the cloudwall or eyewall, which holds the hurricane's most violent winds.

In the calm of the hurricane's eye, a ship's rigging and decks can become crowded with birds, exhausted from battling the fierce winds.

In 1495, the town of Isabella, founded by Columbus on Hispaniola Island, was destroyed by a hurricane—the first European settlement to meet its end this way. Some people think a hurricane caused the mysterious 1588 disappearance of the Roanoke Island settlement, also called the "lost colony."

In 1886, the town of Indianola, Texas, was destroyed by a hurricane and was never rebuilt. The town was there, then three days later, it was gone forever.

On June 26, 1957, Hurricane Audrey tossed a fishing boat weighing 78 tons into an offshore drilling platform, drowning nine men.

The 1900 Galveston hurricane smashed much of that city. It undermined Galveston's role as a financial capital as well as wreaking terror and havoc on the people who lived there.

Weirdly enough, when a hurricane reaches land, the winds at the surface die off more quickly than the higher-level winds, causing air currents that can become, guess what? A full-fledged tornado.

An 1831 Caribbean hurricane shoved a 400-pound piece of solid lead over 500 yards.

The energy in an average one-day hurricane could power the United States for three years.

In 1978, the Citibank building in New York City had a dangerous, structural flaw. A misunderstanding between the engineer and the contractor had allowed some supports to be bolted, rather than welded. Coincidentally, there was hurricane heading up the East Coast. A small army of welders was hired to work secretly at night. Rumors ran wild—the mysterious glow of welder's torches was visible across the skyline as the flaw was fixed. If Citibank had been blown over, 156 blocks might have been destroyed—the buildings would have fallen like gigantic dominos!

After Hurricane Iniki's damaging winds died down in 1992, eight people died of stress-induced heart attacks, three in damaged buildings or from being hit by debris. Two children died in fires in damaged homes.

1999's Hurricane Mitch was one of the worst western hemisphere disasters ever recorded—only the 1900 Galveston hurricane and one in the late 1700s were as bad. Mitch killed 10,000 people in Honduras and caused about $4 billion in damage, an incredible loss for a small, poor nation.

The Great Hurricane of 1780 ran amok in mid-October. There were two others that year that cost many lives as well. Between the three, there were more than 1,000 people killed.

The hurricane eye creates a strange experience for anyone in its path. First the winds rise and the storm begins to roar and howl. Then, as the first side of the cloudwall passes over, the storm screams, its intensity rising dramatically. Suddenly, the eye passing over brings an eerie calm. People think the storm is over. Then the following edge of the cloudwall advances, bringing super-intense winds again, from the opposite direction.

Ships at sea have sometimes survived a hurricane by staying inside the eye—sailing at the same speed the hurricane is traveling!

Hurricanes are usually about 1,000 miles wide and because of the calm eye at the center, they're one of the easiest weather patterns to spot in satellite photos. Meteorologists have nicknamed them "one-eyed monsters."

In 1989 Hurricane Hugo roared across the northeast Caribbean. It devastated small islands east of Puerto Rico, brushed Puerto Rico itself, then smashed into South Carolina. It caused more than $8 billion damage and killed 82 people, mostly on the islands. People wanted the name Hugo retired from the rotating list of names used for hurricanes, so "Humberto," a Spanish name, replaced it. Humberto was used for the first time in 1995— given to a September storm with 105 mph winds that never touched land.

In 1992, there were so many Pacific tropical cyclones that the entire list of alphabetical names was used up. Meteorologists had to use Greek alphabet letters instead.

A Justice of the Peace in the Florida Keys built a hurricane shelter: a solid concrete foundation with a small concrete house over it, anchored by two huge chains. When the 1935 hurricane hit, his family hid in the shelter, but the winds lifted it, concrete, chains and all, into the air. The concrete cracked and threw the family into the water. They were swept against a small tree. With his daughter's baby buttoned inside his coat, the man made a handhold from his belt. His family clung to each other around the tree, holding the children's heads above water. The wind howled, bending the little tree all night—but it held fast and the family lived!

In the Labor Day 1935 Hurricane, a Florida Keys family thought their house was coming apart in the wind. They stumbled into the yard and clung to a gumbo tree. Tragically, not all of them made it through the night. In the morning, sur-vivors faced a cruel irony. Their house had floated, intact, a mile to the south and washed up on another island. Had they stayed in it, they might have all lived.

During the height of a hurricane, one man tied a length of rope around his waist and dragged a string of people behind him. When the hurricane subsided he untied the knots and separated the living from the dead.

Knowing the calm of the 1935 Labor Day Hurricane's eye would not last long, a man ran from the battered cottage where he had taken shelter to head for a stronger building. He didn't make it. Caught in the rising storm-tide and swept seaward, he rode the swell and ended up in a coconut palm. Something hit him in the head, and he was unconscious until he came to and found himself alive but still tangled in the palm tree, 20 feet above the ground.

In 1969, two dozen residents of beachfront apartments threw a "hurricane party" when the U.S. Weather Bureau predicted Camille's landfall 100 miles to the east. But then Camille changed her plans and swung westward. The storm surge ended the party. Rushing water flooded the ground floors and broke second-story windows. Only one party-goer survived. Swimming out her window, she looked back in time to see the building collapse, then spent the night drifting on the storm tide. She was rescued the next morning in a tree five miles away.

One Thibodaux, Louisiana, child lived through Hurricane Andrew because her mother woke her in the stormy night, calling her to come watch their cat madly chasing its shadow by candlelight. The child got up and headed down the hall—just as a massive tree branch crashed through the ceiling and fell onto her bed.

On the barrier island of Grand Isle, Louisiana, a man whose house was washed away during Hurricane Betsy put his chihuahua in a pail, so she could safely float. Both man and dog survived.

When her home was ruined during the 1900 Galveston Hurricane, a pregnant woman was swept away, clinging to the roof of a wrecked cottage. It crashed into other debris and she was thrown off—landing in a steamer trunk bobbing on the flood waters. The trunk was wind driven over the rushing water, finally smashing against the massive wall of the Ursuline Convent. The woman was pulled inside and her baby was born a few hours later, assisted by the nuns.

Other people were saved by the sisters. One man was naked when rescued. The only dry clothing in the convent was a nun's habit. After the storm subsided, he left dressed as a Sister of Charity.

Fifteen men found shelter from hurricane Camille in a warehouse on the Navy base in Gulfport. When stones came crashing through the big aluminum loading doors, the men hid between pallets of building material weighing several tons. A sudden loud rush of wind blew the warehouse away, but the building material was heavy enough to stay put. In the silence as the storm's eye passed over, an armored personnel carrier took them to a much safer underground shelter.

On Thursday, June 27, 1957, Hurricane Audrey was expected to hit the Texas coast. One man wanted to leave that morning, but his wife persuaded him to wait, unwilling to disturb their seven sleeping children or her parents, who had come to find shelter in their newly built home. When the storm hit, they all huddled in the attic as rising water lifted, then floated the house toward White Lake. When the wind changed direction the house tilted, and the heavy deep freezer slid sideways and collapsed a wall, breaking the house apart. One of the children was lost in the rushing water.

The survivors held onto pieces of the wrecked house. Exposed nails cut them. The screaming wind shredded their clothing and tore two of the children from their grandparents' arms. Terrified of the wind, the family also feared water moccasin snakes they knew the flood had disturbed. They were right to worry.

After the storm subsided and they were floating in water filled with dead animals, mud, and snakes, one of the children was bitten. The father struck out to find help, swimming toward a hunting camp he could see on the shore. The camp buildings were full of snakes and other wildlife that had sought storm-shelter. Getting help from a man he hailed, the father returned to his family in a borrowed boat. The child who had been snake-bitten did not survive the long trip to the hospital.

When their ordeal was over, Hurricane Audrey

had killed four of the family's children, wrecked their home, and injured them all terribly. But the baby of the family survived because his mother had refused to let go of him even though she thought he had already died—he was silent and blue with cold and shock most of the long, terrible ordeal. He is married today with two children of his own.

One island family survived Hurricane Audrey's flood by cutting a hole in the attic roof and scrambling out. The next day they found a water moccasin, trampled to death on the attic floor. None of them had known it was there—or the danger they were in!

At 2:00 A.M. Thursday, a man in Oak Grove, Louisiana, woke to the sound of car horns. By 2:45 A.M., he knew the Gulf waters were rising fast and a hurricane warning was in effect. He got his family into the car—but the water was already too deep. He and his wife—and their five children— waded and swam across seven barbed wire and hurricane fences to the newly built South Cameron Parish high school.

The family of seven joined a family of five on the safest place they could find—an air conditioning unit a few feet below the auditorium ceiling. Hurricane Andrew shrieked as the waters rose. As the families huddled on the four by four foot unit for twelve long, desperate hours, the storm floods came within three feet of their perch.

There were forty people in the building, and all survived—some by clinging to loops of stage curtains thrown over ceiling pipes to keep their heads above water. The new high school was almost completely wrecked.

TALL TALES AND DANGEROUS MYTHS

TRUTH: The rotation of the Earth makes hurricanes turn counterclockwise in the Northern hemisphere and clockwise in the Southern hemisphere.

MYTH: Some people believe that water draining out of a sink or toilet follows the same rules. It doesn't! The circular flow of draining water is determined by the shape of the sink or toilet.

TRUTH AND MYTH AND DECEPTION

There is a con man who fools tourists at the equator by pretending that the current of water in a basin goes clockwise when he is on the north side of the equator, then, when he takes a few steps to cross the imaginary line, that the water reverses and goes counterclockwise. He simply turns around to his left or his right, setting up a flow of the water as he walks. The funny thing is that he has it backwards! The directions he uses in his trick are wrong, but the unsuspecting—and uninformed—tourists tip him anyway!

MYTH: Many people believe that the extreme low pressure in the "eye" of a hurricane allows the ocean to rise in response, causing destructive storm surges.

TRUTH: Storm surge is mostly caused by the winds pushing the water ahead of the storm.

MYTH: The friction over land kills hurricanes.

TRUTH: After just a few hours, a hurricane over land will begin to weaken rapidly—not because of friction—but because the storm lacks the moisture and heat sources that the ocean provided.

MYTH: Big hurricanes are the worst.

TRUTH: There is little connection between intensity and size. Hurricane Andrew was not big, but it was ferocious.

MYTH: During a hurricane, close windows and doors on the storm side and open them on the lee side—or your house might explode.

TRUTH: All of the doors and windows should be closed (and shuttered) during a hurricane. The pressure difference between inside and outside is not dangerous. Wind-driven debris flying through an open window is.

MYTH: You should tape your windows when a hurricane threatens.

TRUTH: Taping windows is a waste of effort, time, and tape. Shutters afford some protection—tape simply isn't strong enough.

THE NAME GAME

Hurricane names are all chosen from the World Meteorological Organization's list. There are six lists for the Atlantic, used one per year until, every sixth year, the first list is used again. The names are alphabetic. The first hurricane of the year will start with the letter A, the next with B, and so on. Letters Q, U, X, Y, and Z aren't used.

Hurricanes last a week or more, and there's often more than one in an area at once. The names make it easier for people to track the storms as they listen to forecasts, hurricane watches, and warnings.

Naming hurricanes started so long ago no one knows where or why it began. There was an Australian forecaster early in the twentieth century who named the deadly storms after the wives of politicians he didn't like! He made fun of them by saying their names during storm reports, then finishing the sentence with " . . . is causing great distress" or " . . . is wandering aimlessly about the Pacific."

During World War II, tropical cyclones were nicknamed, often using the names of the wives and girlfriends of U.S. Army Air Corp and Navy meteorologists. Then, from 1950 to 1952, tropical cyclones of the North Atlantic Ocean were labeled Able-Baker-Charlie-etc., using the Army's phonetic alphabet. In 1953 the U.S. Weather Bureau switched to women's names. In 1979, meteorologists switched to using alternating men's and women's names—as well as names in French and Spanish in addition to English.

Some hurricane names are retired, not to be reused for at least ten years. The most-affected country can request a storm's name be removed from use.

Here are the name lists for Atlantic, Caribbean Sea, and Gulf of Mexico storms for 2000 and 2001. Is your name going to be used for a Hurricane soon?

2000	2001
Alberto	Allison
Beryl	Barry
Chris	Chantal
Debby	Dean
Ernesto	Erin
Florence	Felix
Gordon	Gabrielle
Helene	Humberto
Isaac	Iris
Joyce	Jerry
Keith	Karen
Leslie	Lorenzo
Michael	Michelle
Nadine	Noel
Oscar	Olga
Patty	Pablo
Rafael	Rebekah
Sandy	Sebastian
Tony	Tanya
Valerie	Van
William	Wendy

When a storm name is retired, member countries of the World Meteorological Organization from that region select a new name in English, French, or Spanish—these are the languages of storm victims of Atlantic hurricanes.

HOW BAD WAS IT: SCALES AND MEASURES

We label hurricanes (or tropical cyclones or whatever the storm is called in its native ocean neighborhood) according to the speed of the winds near the center of the storm:

- A tropical depression has winds of 38 miles per hour or less
- A tropical storm has winds of 39 to 73 miles per hour. At this point it is assigned a name.
- A hurricane (by any name) has winds of 74 miles per hour or more.

There are three types of damage caused by hurricanes:

Wind Damage: Hurricane-force winds are 74 mph or more and often extend far inland. Winds that strong damage poorly constructed buildings and mobile homes. Signs, roofing material, siding, and household or industrial debris are hurtled along with the wind and can injure anyone caught in the open. Hurricane winds can get strong enough to demolish even well-built buildings, and being outside can be extremely dangerous.

Storm Surge Damage: A storm surge is a dome-shaped swell of lake or sea water, often 50 to 100 miles wide, that sweeps across the coastline as a hurricane makes landfall. This already flood-high water is topped by waves. The stronger the hurricane and the shallower the offshore water, the higher the surge will be. For those who live on a coast, the storm surge is a serious threat to life and property.

Flood Damage: Widespread torrential rains—often more than six inches in a short time span, cause destructive and life-threatening floods—a major threat to inland areas during a hurricane.

Hurricanes are rated from one to five on the Saffir-Simpson Hurricane Scale. The rating is an estimate of the hurricane's intensity and its potential to do these four kinds of damage:

Wind Speed/ Miles per Hour	Storm Surge	Damage
1. 74–95	4–5 feet	Minimal
2. 96–110	6–8 feet	Moderate
3. 111–130	9–12 feet	Extensive
4. 131–155	13–18 feet	Extreme
5. More than 155	More than 18 feet	Catastrophic

Category 1: Damage is mostly to trees, foliage, and unanchored buildings and mobile homes. There is some damage to piers and poorly constructed signs. Low-lying coastal roads are flooded. Small craft in exposed anchorage might be torn from moorings.

Category 2: There is worse damage to trees and shrubs (some trees are down) and major damage to piers, exposed un-anchored structures, and poorly constructed signs. There is some damage to roofs, windows, and doors, but no major damage to anchored buildings. Coast roads and low-lying routes inland are flooded two to four hours before arrival of the hurricane center. Marinas are flooded. Small craft in unprotected anchorages are torn from moorings. Some coastal homes and lowlands are evacuated.

Category 3: Tree leaves are stripped; big trees

and most poorly built signs are blown down. Some roofs, windows, and doors are damaged. There is some structural damage to small buildings. Mobile homes are destroyed. Coastal flooding is serious, with many smaller structures destroyed. Bigger coastal buildings are damaged by battering waves and floating debris. Low-lying areas and escape routes are flooded by three to five hours before the hurricane center arrives. Low areas inland to eight miles are flooded. Residences within several blocks of beach might be evacuated.

Category 4: Shrubs and trees are blown down; all signs are down. There is extensive damage to roofing, windows, and doors, complete roof failure on smaller structures and complete destruction of mobile homes. Flat lowland is flooded inland as far as 10 miles. There is major flood damage to lower floors of shoreline buildings, plus damage from battering waves and floating debris. Low-lying escape routes are flooded three to five hours before the hurricane center arrives. There is major beach sand erosion. There might be massive evacuation of homes within 500 yards of shore, and possibly of single-story homes within two miles of shore.

Category 5: There is very severe window and door damage, and complete roof failure on many buildings. Mobile homes and some buildings are completely destroyed. Small structures are overturned or blown away. There is major damage to lower floors of all structures less than 15 feet above sea level within 500 yards of shore. Low-lying escape routes inland are flooded three to five hours before the hurricane center arrives. Massive evacuation of residential areas on low ground within five to 10 miles of shore is possible.

A Category 2 hurricane isn't just twice as bad as a Category 1—it's 10 times as destructive! Here's how the scale works:

Category 2	10 times as destructive as Category 1
Category 3	50 times as destructive as Category 2
Category 4	100 times as destructive as Category 3
Category 5	250 times as destructive as Category 4

Storms in Categories 3, 4, and 5 make up only 21% of all U.S. hurricanes but are responsible for 83% of all of the damage. They are MUCH more powerful. A Category 4 or greater hurricane crosses the U.S. coastline about once every six years.

The birth of a hurricane requires at least three conditions:

1. The ocean water must be at least 80 degrees F on the surface. A hurricane is like a huge heat engine, and it needs fuel.

2. Atmospheric moisture from sea water evaporation must combine with that heat and energy.

3. A spiraling wind pattern must form near the ocean surface.

Bands of thunderstorms form and warm the air further. It rises higher into the atmosphere. If the winds at these higher levels are fairly light, this structure of rising warm air remains intact and grows stronger: the beginnings of a hurricane.

Thunderstorms can move offshore and over warm water—and form deadly hurricanes. Some of the worst start as squall lines over Western Africa, then move west off the coast. If the water below is warm enough, they can intensify into hurricanes.

Hurricanes don't form outside warm climate zones, because the oceans are too cold.

The earth's rotation sets up the *Coriolis force,*

which pulls winds counterclockwise in the Northern Hemisphere and clockwise in the Southern Hemisphere. Hurricanes formed in the Atlantic Ocean are blown toward North America. Hurricanes from the Pacific Ocean are called typhoons and blow toward Asia. An average of 10 of these storms form over the Atlantic Ocean, Caribbean Sea, or Gulf of Mexico each year. About six of these will strengthen enough to become hurricanes.

Hurricanes are "steered" and moved along by the envelope of wind currents around the storm— all the way from the earth's surface up to 50,000 feet or more. If these currents are strong, it's easier to predict where the hurricane will go. When they're weak, hurricanes seem to move whimsically and are impossible to predict.

No one knows why some hurricanes suddenly die when conditions seem perfect for them. But there is one known hurricane killer: a storm hitting the cooler surface of land or of cold water will dissipate. Without a steady supply of heat, hurricanes can't last.

Hurricane season begins June 1. The worst storms are usually in August and September, when ocean water is warmest. The odds against hurricanes forming rises with water temperatures, until the official end of hurricane season on November 30.

There is an old sailor's poem about hurricane season:

June too soon.
July stand by.
August look out you must.
September remember.
October all over.

Most Powerful (20th Century)

1. (Gilbert) Caribbean and Gulf of Mexico, 1988; 218 mph.
2. (Camille) Mississippi, 1969; 201 mph.
3. Labor Day Hurricane, Florida Keys, 1935; 200 mph (estimate).
4. (Andrew) Florida and Louisiana, 1992; 144 mph.

Deadliest in the U.S.

1. (Unnamed) Galveston Texas, June, 1900. Over 8,000 deaths. The city was totally leveled when the violent storm suddenly appeared and destroyed the only bridge to high ground. This hurricane killed more people than any other natural disaster in United States history.
2. (San Felipe) Lake Okeechobee, Florida, September, 1928. Over 2,000 deaths.
3. (Unnamed) Florida Keys and South Texas, September, 1919. Over 900 deaths.
4. (Unnamed) New England and Long Island, September, 1938. 600 deaths.
5. (Unnamed) Florida Keys, September, 1935. 408 deaths.

6. (Audrey) Louisiana and Texas, June, 1957. 390 deaths.

7. (Unnamed) Northeastern U.S., September, 1944. 388 deaths, mostly on ships at sea.

8. (Unnamed) Grand Isle, Louisiana, September, 1909. 350 deaths.

9. (Unnamed) New Orleans, Louisiana, August, 1959. 279 deaths.

10. (Camille) Mississippi, Louisiana, Alabama, Virginia, and West Virginia. 256 deaths.

Deadliest Atlantic 1492-2000

1. (Unnamed) Lesser Antilles, October, 1780. More than 22,000 deaths, plus thousands more offshore.

2. (Unnamed) Galveston, Texas, June, 1900. More than 8,000 deaths. The city was destroyed, including the only bridge to high ground.

3. (Fifi) Honduras, September, 1974. 8,000–10,000 deaths.

4. (Unnamed) Dominican Republic, September, 1930. 8,000 deaths.

5. (Flora) Haiti and Cuba, September, 1963. 8,000 deaths.

6. (Unnamed) Pointe-a-Pitre Bay, Guatemala. September, 1776. 6,000 deaths.

7. (Unnamed) Newfoundland Banks,

September, 1775. 4,000 deaths.

8. (Unnamed) Puerto Rico, Carolinas, August, 1899. 3,433 deaths.

9. (Unnamed) Florida, Guatemala, Puerto Rico. September, 1928. 3,411 deaths.

10. (Unnamed) Cuba, Jamaica, November, 1932. 3,107 deaths.

MOST DAMAGING STORM

The worst U.S. hurricane damage was inflicted by the 1926 Great Miami Hurricane. If this storm had hit in the mid-1990s, it would have caused an estimated $63 billion in damage in South Florida and then an additional $9 billion in the Florida panhandle and Alabama.

LIFESAVING FACTS

Be alert for radio or TV weather updates and warnings. Stay in touch with your neighbors about coming danger. Plan a place to meet your family in case you are separated. Choose a friend or relative out of state for your family members to call to leave messages.

Assemble a disaster kit. (See Chapter Two)

Store extra water. Check to make sure you have enough food.

Storm shutters are the best protection for windows. If your house does not have them, help an adult board up windows with 5/8-inch marine plywood. Tape does NOT prevent windows from breaking.

Bring in outside furniture. An adult should remove roof antennas, if possible. Help an adult shut off your utilities—water, electricity, and gas. Make sure there is gas in the car and be ready to evacuate immediately, if you are told to do so.

If you don't need to evacuate, be sure to STAY INDOORS during a hurricane. You can be killed by flying debris. Don't be fooled by a lull—it could be the eye of the storm. Stay close to shelter.

If you do evacuate, do NOT go home until officials say it is safe.

Flying through a hurricane is a great way to get data on its strength and movement so people can be warned. Having time to seek shelter or flee saves many lives. These hurricane flights are dangerous and exciting, and are an accepted part of storm-study.

If the storms enter the Caribbean Sea and approach the U.S., brave pilots and crews fly planes into the storms to measure exact location, size, storm surge height, direction of travel, and wind speed. This information will determine warnings issued to people whose lives are at stake. Crews sometimes use the eye of the storm to transmit storm data to the National Hurricane Center through direct satellite communications.

But you have to wonder—who was brave enough to try it the first time? On July 27, 1943, Air Force Colonel Joseph B. Duckworth, commander of the Air Force's instrument flight training school at Bryan, Texas, flew through a hurricane on a dare.

British pilots in training had insulted Duckworth's AT-6 airplane. He countered by claiming he could fly it into a hurricane. Bets were placed. Duckworth and another flyer named O'Hair took off, then radioed Houston flight controllers, just as the storm's static cut them off.

The AT-6 was battered ferociously, tossed up and down thousands of feet by severe updrafts and downdrafts. Then Duckworth and O'Hair suddenly entered the calm, quiet eye of the storm and were the first men to see the towering white cloudwalls—with blue sky above, and the flat Texas plains below.

They tried to stay within the eye, but couldn't, and plunged back into another wild ride. They managed to land safely, hours later. Airborne reconnaissance of hurricanes had begun.

Today, the National Hurricane Center in Coral Gables, Florida monitors forming hurricanes using satellite photographs and sophisticated radar. They use WP-3s, high-performance airplanes—flying labs equipped with measuring and sampling instruments. NASA is also designing and developing Earth remote sensing spacecraft to track these storms.

FRIGHTFULLY FUNNY AND SERIOUSLY STRANGE

During the height of Hurricane Iniki on Kawai in Hawaii, two men stole a grocery store safe. They got it outside, but the hurricane kept knocking them down. They finally left the safe standing in the middle of the street. Local survivors joked that the two "didn't know another way to keep safe in a storm."

After a disaster, phone lines are often down. Many Iniki survivors couldn't find paper in their wrecked homes to write letters to worried friends and family. Some of them wrote short funny messages on coconuts and the Post Office mailed them.

Hurricane Audrey deposited a shrimp boat named *Audrey* in the top of an oak tree. At Little Chenier, Louisiana, she sank a tug boat named *Audrey*. People joked that she didn't like rival Audreys.

After Hurricane Camille's storm surge hit the Ramada Inn in Long Beach, Mississippi, the building looked as if it were built on stilts. There wasn't anything left on the bottom floor.

A TV newsman stood on a shore being pounded by Hurricane Camille, warning people to evacuate. TV viewers could see the huge menacing waves in the background—and the surfers riding them.

There was enough debris from Hurricane Andrew in South Florida to make a pile over 300 stories high. Entrepreneurs sorted out and sold tons of aluminum siding, lawn chairs, and awnings as salvage. For a while, some people made up to $1,000 a day.

During Hurricane Andrew, someone at the National Hurricane Center in Coral Gables, Florida reported: "I don't know how fast the wind is blowing. The wind speed indicator blew away."

The survivors of Hurricane Iniki were often frustrated by the difficulty of finding temporary housing, and being advised to "relax" didn't help much. When a counselor told one man he was too tense, the man replied, "No, I'm NOT too tense. I NEED two tents!"

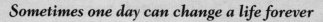

Sometimes one day can change a life forever

American Diaries

**Different girls,
living in different periods of America's past,
reveal their hearts' secrets in the pages
of their diaries. Each one faces a challenge
that will change her life forever.
Don't miss any of their stories:**

The past comes ALIVE
in stirring historical fiction
from
ALADDIN PAPERBACKS

☐ **The Best Bad Thing**
Yoshiko Uchida
0-689-71745-8
$4.99 US
$6.99 Canadian

☐ **Brothers of the Heart**
Joan W. Blos
0-689-71724-5
$4.99 US
$6.99 Canadian

☐ **Caddie Woodlawn**
Carol Ryrie Brink
0-689-71370-3
$4.99 US
$6.99 Canadian

☐ **The Eternal Spring of Mr. Ito**
Sheila Garrigue
0-689-71809-8
$4.99 US
$6.99 Canadian

☐ **Forty Acres and Maybe a Mule**
Harriette Gillem Robinet
0-689-83317-2
$4.99 US
$6.99 Canadian

☐ **A Gathering of Days**
Joan W. Blos
0-689-71419-X
$4.99 US
$6.99 Canadian

☐ **Hope**
Louann Gaeddert
0-689-80382-6
$3.99 US
$4.99 Canadian

☐ **A Jar of Dreams**
Yoshiko Uchida
0-689-71672-9
$4.99 US
$6.99 Canadian

☐ **The Journey Home**
Yoshiko Uchida
0-689-71641-9
$4.99 US
$6.99 Canadian

☐ **The Journey to America Saga**
Sonia Levitin
Annie's Promise
0-689-80440-7
Journey to America
0-689-71130-1
Silver Days
0-689-71570-6
All $4.99 US
$6.99 Canadian

☐ **The Second Mrs. Giaconda**
E. L. Konigsburg
0-689-82121-2
$4.50 US
$5.99 Canadian

☐ **Shades of Gray**
Carolyn Reeder
0-689-82696-6
$4.99 US
$6.99 Canadian

☐ **Steal Away Home**
Lois Ruby
0-689-82435-1
$4.50 US
$6.50 Canadian

☐ **Under the Shadow of Wings**
Sara Harrell Banks
0-689-82436-X
$4.99 US
$6.99 Canadian

Aladdin Paperbacks • Simon & Schuster Children's Publishing • www.SimonSaysKids.com